D1429019

THE CHILDREN'S GOLDEN LIBRARY
40

The Children's Golden Library

40

Little House on the Prairie
Laura Ingalls Wilder

First published in 1935

Text copyright © 1935 Laura Ingalls Wilder
Copyright renewed © 1963 Roger L. MacBrider
© 2000 Egmont Books Limited

Published © 2004 MDS BOOKS/ MEDIASAT in association with Mediafund Ltd.
for this edition.

Original Design © Mediasat Group
Cover Illustration Copyright © Juan Lobatón Scott

ISBN   84-9789-481-2
Dep. legal B-11 082-2004

Printed and bound in Spain
by Printer Industria Gráfica, Barcelona

www.mediasatgroup.com

LAURA INGALLS
WILDER
Little House
on the Prairie

THE CHILDREN'S GOLDEN LIBRARY

1

Going West

A long time ago, when all the grandfathers and grandmoth-ers of today were little boys and little girls or very small babies, or perhaps not even born, Pa and Ma and Mary and Laura and Baby Carrie left their little house in the Big Woods of Wisconsin. They drove away and left it lonely and empty in the clearing among the big trees, and they never saw that little house again.

They were going to the Indian country.

Pa said there were too many people in the Big Woods now. Quite often Laura heard the ringing thud of an axe which was not Pa's axe, or the echo of a shot that did not come from his gun. The path that went by the little house had become a road. Almost every day Laura and Mary stopped their playing and stared in surprise at a wagon slowly creaking by on that road.

Wild animals would not stay in a country where there were so many people. Pa did not like to stay, either. He liked a country where the wild animals lived without being afraid. He liked to see the little fawns and their mothers looking at him from the shadowy woods, and the fat, lazy bears eating berries in the wild-berry patches.

In the long winter evenings he talked to Ma about the Western country. In the West the land was level, and there were no trees. The grass grew thick and high. There the wild animals wandered and fed as though they were in a pasture that stretched much farther than a man could see, and there were no settlers. Only Indians lived there.

One day in the very last of the winter Pa said to Ma, 'Seeing you don't object, I've decided to go see the West. I've had an offer for this place, and we can sell it now for as much as we're ever likely to get, enough to give us a start in a new country.'

'Oh, Charles, must we go now?' Ma said. The weather was so cold and the snug house was so comfortable.

'If we are going this year, we must go now,' said Pa. 'We can't get across the Mississippi after the ice breaks.'

So Pa sold the little house. He sold the cow and calf. He made hickory bows and fastened them upright to the wagon box. Ma helped him stretch white canvas over them.

In the thin dark morning Ma gently shook Mary and Laura till they got up. In firelight and candlelight she washed and combed them and dressed them warmly. Over their long red flannel underwear she put wool petticoats and wool dresses and long wool stockings. She put their coats on them, and their rabbit-skin hoods and their red yarn mittens.

Everything from the little house was in the wagon, except the beds and tables and chairs. They did not need to take these, because Pa could always make new ones.

There was thin snow on the ground. The air was still and cold and dark. The bare trees stood up against the frosty stars. But in the east the sky was pale and through the grey woods came lanterns with wagons and horses, bringing Grandpa and Grandma and aunts and uncles and cousins.

Mary and Laura clung tight to their rag dolls and did not say anything. The cousins stood around and looked at them. Grandma and all the aunts hugged and kissed them and hugged and kissed them again, saying good-bye.

Pa hung his gun to the wagon bows inside the canvas top, where he could reach it quickly from the seat. He hung his bullet-pouch and powder-horn beneath it. He laid the fiddle-box carefully between pillows, where jolting would not hurt the fiddle.

The uncles helped him hitch the horses to the wagon. All the cousins were told to kiss Mary and Laura, so they did. Pa picked up Mary and then Laura, and set them on the bed in the back of the wagon. He helped Ma climb up to the wagon seat, and Grandma reached up and gave her Baby Carrie. Pa swung up and sat beside Ma, and Jack, the brindle bulldog, went under the wagon.

So they all went away from the little log house. The shutters were over the windows, so the little house could not see them go. It stayed there inside the log fence, behind the two big oak trees that in the summertime had made green roofs for Mary and Laura to play under. And that was the last of the little house.

Pa promised that when they came to the West, Laura should see a papoose.

'What is a papoose?' she asked him, and he said, 'A papoose is a little, brown, Indian baby.'

They drove a long way through the snowy woods, till they came to the town of Pepin. Mary and Laura had seen it once before, but it looked different now. The door of the store and the doors of all the houses were shut, the stumps were covered with snow, and no little children were playing outdoors. Big cords of wood stood among the stumps. Only two or three men in boots and fur caps and bright plaid coats were to be seen.

Ma and Laura and Mary ate bread and molasses in the wagon, and the horses ate corn from nosebags, while inside the store Pa traded his furs for things they would need on the journey. They could not stay long in the town, because they must cross the lake that day.

The enormous lake stretched flat and smooth and white all the way to the edge of the grey sky. Wagon tracks went away across it, so far that you could not see where they went; they ended in nothing at all.

Pa drove the wagon out on to the ice, following those wagon tracks. The horses' hoofs clop-clopped with a dull sound, the wagon wheels went crunching. The town grew smaller and smaller behind, till even the tall store was only a dot. All around the wagon there was nothing but empty and silent space. Laura didn't like it. But Pa was on the wagon seat and Jack was under the wagon; she knew that nothing could hurt her while Pa and Jack were there.

At last the wagon was pulling up a slope of earth again, and again there were trees. There was a little log house, too, among the trees. So Laura felt better.

Nobody lived in the little house; it was a place to camp in. It was a tiny house, and strange, with a big fireplace and rough bunks against all the walls. But it was warm when Pa had built a fire in the fireplace. That night Mary and Laura and Baby Carrie slept with Ma in a bed made on the floor before the fire, while Pa slept outside in the wagon, to guard it and the horses.

In the night a strange noise wakened Laura. It sounded like a shot, but it was sharper and longer than a shot. Again and again she heard it. Mary and Carrie were asleep, but Laura couldn't sleep until Ma's voice came softly through the dark. 'Go to sleep, Laura,' Ma said. 'It's only the ice cracking.'

Next morning Pa said, 'It's lucky we crossed yesterday, Caroline. Wouldn't wonder if the ice broke up today. We made a late crossing, and we're lucky it didn't start breaking up while we were out in the middle of it.'

'I thought about that yesterday, Charles,' Ma replied, gently.

Laura hadn't thought about it before, but now she

thought what would have happened if the ice had cracked under the wagon wheels and they had all gone down into the cold water in the middle of that vast lake.

'You're frightening somebody, Charles,' Ma said, and Pa caught Laura up in his safe, big hug.

'We're across the Mississippi!' he said, hugging her joyously. 'How do you like that, little half-pint of sweet cider half drunk up? Do you like going out west where Indians live?'

Laura said she liked it, and she asked if they were in the Indian country now. But they were not; they were in Minnesota.

It was a long, long way to Indian territory. Almost every day the horses travelled as far as they could; almost every night Pa and Ma made camp in a new place. Sometimes they had to stay several days in one camp because a creek was in flood and they couldn't cross it till the water went down. They crossed too many creeks to count. They saw strange woods and hills, and stranger country with no trees. They drove across rivers on long wooden bridges, and they came to one wide yellow river that had no bridge.

That was the Missouri River. Pa drove on to a raft, and they all sat still in the wagon while the raft went swaying away from the safe land and slowly crossed all that rolling muddy-yellow water.

After more days they came to hills again. In a valley the wagon stuck fast in deep black mud. Rain poured down and thunder crashed and lightning flared. There was no place to make camp and build a fire. Everything was damp and cold and miserable in the wagon, but they had to stay in it and eat cold bits of food.

Next day Pa found a place on a hillside where they could camp. The rain had stopped, but they had to wait a week before the creek went down and the mud dried so that Pa could dig the wagon wheels out of it and go on.

One day, while they were waiting, a tall, lean man came out of the woods, riding a black pony. He and Pa talked awhile, then they went off into the woods together, and when they came back, both of them were riding black ponies. Pa had traded the tired brown horses for those ponies.

They were beautiful little horses, and Pa said they were not really ponies; they were western mustangs. 'They're strong as mules and gentle as kittens,' Pa said. They had large, soft, gentle eyes, and long manes and tails, and slender legs and feet much smaller and quicker than the feet of horses in the Big Woods.

When Laura asked what their names were, Pa said that she and Mary could name them. So Mary named one, Pet, and Laura named the other, Patty. When the creek's roar was not so loud and the road was drier, Pa dug the wagon out of the mud. He hitched Pet and Patty to it, and they all went on together.

They had come in the covered wagon all the long way from the Big Woods of Wisconsin, across Minnesota and Iowa and Missouri. All that long way, Jack had trotted under the wagon. Now they set out to go across Kansas.

Kansas was an endless flat land covered with tall grass blowing in the wind. Day after day they travelled in Kansas, and saw nothing but the rippling grass and the enormous sky. In a perfect circle the sky curved down to the level land, and the wagon was in the circle's exact middle.

All day long Pet and Patty went forward, trotting and walking and trotting again, but they couldn't get out of the middle of that circle. When the sun went down, the circle was still around them and the edge of the sky was pink. Then slowly the land became black. The wind made a lonely sound in the grass. The camp fire was small and lost in so much space. But large stars hung from the sky, glittering so near that Laura felt she could almost touch them.

Next day the land was the same, the sky was the same, the circle did not change. Laura and Mary were tired of them all. There was nothing new to do and nothing new to look at. The bed was made in the back of the wagon and neatly covered with a grey blanket; Laura and Mary sat on it. The canvas sides of the wagon-top were rolled up and tied, so the prairie wind blew in. It whipped Laura's straight brown hair and Mary's golden curls every-which-way, and the strong light screwed up their eyelids.

Sometimes a big jack rabbit bounded in big bounds away over the blowing grass. Jack paid no attention. Poor Jack was tired, too, and his paws were sore from travelling so far. The wagon kept on jolting, the canvas top snapped in the wind. Two faint wheel tracks kept going away behind the wagon, always the same.

Pa's back was hunched. The reins were loose in his hands, the wind blew his long brown beard. Ma sat straight and quiet, her hands folded in her lap. Baby Carrie slept in a nest among the soft bundles.

'Ah-wow!' Mary yawned, and Laura said: 'Ma, can't we get out and run behind the wagon? My legs are so tired.'

'No, Laura,' Ma Said.

'Aren't we going to camp pretty soon?' Laura asked. It seemed such a long time since noon, when they had eaten their lunch sitting on the clean grass in the shade of the wagon.

Pa answered: 'Not yet. It's too early to camp now.'

'I want to camp, now! I'm so tired,' Laura said.

Then Ma said, 'Laura.' That was all, but it meant that Laura must not complain. So she did not complain any more out loud, but she was still naughty, inside. She sat and thought complaints to herself.

Her legs ached and the wind wouldn't stop blowing her hair. The grass waved and the wagon jolted and nothing else happened for a long time.

'We're coming to a creek or a river,' Pa said. 'Girls, can you see those trees ahead?'

Laura stood up and held to one of the wagon bows. Far ahead she saw a low dark smudge. 'That's trees,' Pa said. 'You can tell by the shape of the shadows. In this country, trees mean water. That's where we'll camp tonight.'

2

Crossing the Creek

Pet and Patty began to trot briskly, as if they were glad, too. Laura held tight to the wagon bow and stood up in the jolting wagon. Beyond Pa's shoulder and far across the waves of green grass she could see the trees, and they were not like any trees she had seen before. They were no taller than bushes.

'Whoa!' said Pa, suddenly. 'Now which way?' he muttered to himself.

The road divided here, and you could not tell which was the more-travelled way. Both of them were faint wheel tracks in the grass. One went towards the west, the other sloped downward a little, towards the south. Both soon vanished in the tall, blowing grass.

'Better go downhill, I guess,' Pa decided. 'The creek's down in the bottoms. Must be this is the way to the ford.' He turned Pet and Patty towards the south.

The road went down and up and down and up again, over gently curving land. The trees were nearer now, but they were no taller. Then Laura gasped and clutched the wagon bow, for almost under Pet's and Patty's noses there was no more blowing grass, there was no land at all. She looked beyond the edge of the land and across the tops of trees.

The road turned there. For a little way it went along the

cliff's top, then it went sharply downward. Pa put on the brakes; Pet and Patty braced themselves backward and almost sat down. The wagon wheels slid onward, little by little lowering the wagon farther down the steep slope into the ground. Jagged cliffs of bare red earth rose up on both sides of the wagon. Grass waved along their tops, but nothing grew on their seamed, straight-up-and-down sides. They were hot, and heat came from them against Laura's face. The wind was still blowing overhead, but it did not blow down into this deep crack in the ground. The stillness seemed strange and empty.

Then once more the wagon was level. The narrow crack down which it had come opened into the bottom lands. Here grew the tall trees whose tops Laura had seen from the prairie above. Shady groves were scattered on the rolling meadows, and in the groves deer were lying down, hardly to be seen among the shadows. The deer turned their heads towards the wagon, and curious fawns stood up to see it more clearly.

Laura was surprised because she did not see the creek. But the bottom lands were wide. Down here, below the prairie, there were gentle hills and open sunny places. The air was still and hot. Under the wagon wheels the ground was soft. In the sunny open spaces the grass grew thin, and deer had cropped it short.

For a while the high, bare cliffs of red earth stood up behind the wagon. But they were almost hidden behind hills and trees when Pet and Patty stopped to drink from the creek.

The rushing sound of the water filled the still air. All along the creek banks the trees hung over it and made it dark with shadows. In the middle it ran swiftly, sparkling silver and blue.

'This creek's pretty high,' Pa said. 'But I guess we can make it all right. You can see this is a ford, by the old wheel ruts. What do you say, Caroline?'

'Whatever you say, Charles,' Ma answered.

Pet and Patty lifted their wet noses. They pricked their ears forward, looking at the creek; then they pricked them backward to hear what Pa would say. They sighed and laid their soft noses together to whisper to each other. A little way upstream, Jack was lapping the water with his red tongue.

'I'll tie down the wagon-cover,' Pa said. He climbed down from the seat, unrolled the canvas sides and tied them firmly to the wagon box. Then he pulled the rope at the back, so that the canvas puckered together in the middle, leaving only a tiny round hole, too small to see through.

Mary huddled down on the bed. She did not like fords; she was afraid of the rushing water. But Laura was excited; she liked the splashing. Pa climbed to the seat, saying, 'They may have to swim, out there in the middle. But we'll make it all right, Caroline.'

Laura thought of Jack and said, 'I wish Jack could ride in the wagon, Pa.'

Pa did not answer. He gathered the reins tightly in his hands. Ma said, 'Jack can swim, Laura. He will be all right.'

The wagon went forward softly in mud. Water began to splash against the wheels. The splashing grew louder. The wagon shook as the noisy water struck at it. Then all at once the wagon lifted and balanced and swayed. It was a lovely feeling.

The noise stopped, and Ma said, sharply, 'Lie down, girls!'

Quick as a flash, Mary and Laura dropped flat on the bed. When Ma spoke like that, they did as they were told. Ma's arm pulled a smothering blanket over them, heads and all.

'Be still, just as you are. Don't move!' she said.

Mary did not move; she was trembling and still. But Laura could not help wriggling a little bit. She did so want to see what was happening. She could feel the wagon swaying and turning; the splashing was noisy again, and again it died away. Then Pa's voice frightened Laura. It said, 'Take them, Caroline!'

The wagon lurched; there was a sudden heavy splash beside it. Laura sat straight up and clawed the blanket from her head.

Pa was gone. Ma sat alone, holding tight to the reins with both hands. Mary hid her face in the blanket again, but Laura rose up farther. She couldn't see the creek bank. She couldn't see anything in front of the wagon but water rushing at it. And in the water, three heads; Pet's head and Patty's head and Pa's small, wet head. Pa's fist in the water was holding tight to Pet's bridle.

Laura could faintly hear Pa's voice through the rushing of the water. It sounded calm and cheerful, but she couldn't hear what he said. He was talking to the horses. Ma's face was white and scared.

'Lie down, Laura,' Ma said.

Laura lay down. She felt cold and sick. Her eyes were shut tight, but she could still see the terrible water and Pa's brown beard drowning in it.

For a long, long time the wagon swayed and swung, and Mary cried without making a sound, and Laura's stomach felt sicker and sicker. Then the front wheels struck and grated, and Pa shouted. The whole wagon jerked and jolted and tipped backward, but the wheels were turning on the ground. Laura was up again, holding to the seat; she saw Pet's and Patty's scrambling wet backs climbing a steep bank, and Pa running beside them, shouting, 'Hi, Patty! Hi, Pet! Get up! Get up! Whoopsy-daisy! Good girls!'

At the top of the bank they stood still, panting and dripping. And the wagon stood still, safely out of that creek.

Pa stood panting and dripping, too, and Ma said, 'Oh, Charles!'

'There, there, Caroline,' said Pa. 'We're all safe, thanks to a good tight wagon-box well fastened to the running-gear.

I never saw a creek rise so fast in my life. Pet and Patty are good swimmers, but I guess they wouldn't have made it if I hadn't helped them.'

If Pa had not known what to do, or if Ma had been too frightened to drive, or if Laura and Mary had been naughty and bothered her, then they would all have been lost. The river would have rolled them over and over and carried them away and drowned them, and nobody would ever have known what became of them. For weeks, perhaps, no other person would come along that road.

'Well,' said Pa, 'all's well that ends well,' and Ma said, 'Charles, you're wet to the skin.'

Before Pa could answer, Laura cried, 'Oh, where's Jack?'

They had forgotten Jack. They had left him on the other side of that dreadful water and now they could not see him anywhere. He must have tried to swim after them, but they could not see him struggling in the water now.

Laura swallowed hard, to keep from crying. She knew it was shameful to cry, but there was crying inside her. All the long way from Wisconsin poor Jack had followed them so patiently and faithfully, and now they had left him to drown. He was so tired, and they might have taken him into the wagon. He had stood on the bank and seen the wagon going away from him, as if they didn't care for him at all. And he would never know how much they wanted him.

Pa said he wouldn't have done such a thing to Jack, not for a million dollars. If he'd known how that creek would rise when they were in midstream, he would never have let Jack try to swim it. 'But that can't be helped now,' he said.

He went far up and down the creek bank, looking for Jack, calling him and whistling for him.

It was no use. Jack was gone.

At last there was nothing to do but to go on. Pet and Patty were rested. Pa's clothes had dried on him while he searched for Jack. He took the reins again, and drove uphill, out of the river bottoms.

Laura looked back all the way. She knew she wouldn't see Jack again, but she wanted to. She didn't see anything but low curves of land coming between the wagon and the creek, and beyond the creek those strange cliffs of red earth rose up again.

Then other bluffs just like them stood up in front of the wagon. Faint wheel tracks went into a crack between those earthen walls. Pet and Patty climbed till the crack became a small grassy valley. And the valley widened out to the High Prairie once more.

No road, not even the faintest trace of wheels or of a rider's passing, could be seen anywhere. That prairie looked as if no human eye had ever seen it before. Only the tall wild grass covered the endless empty land and a great empty sky arched over it. Far away the sun's edge touched the rim of the earth. The sun was enormous and it was throbbing and pulsing with light. All around the sky's edge ran a pale pink glow, and above the pink was yellow, and above that blue. Above the blue the sky was no colour at all. Purple shadows were gathering over the land, and the wind was mourning.

Pa stopped the mustangs. He and Ma got out of the wagon to make camp, and Mary and Laura climbed down to the ground, too.

'Oh, Ma,' Laura begged, 'Jack has gone to heaven, hasn't he? He was such a good dog, can't he go to heaven?'

Ma did not know what to answer, but Pa said: 'Yes, Laura, he can. God that doesn't forget the sparrows won't leave a good dog like Jack out in the cold.'

Laura felt only a little better. She was not happy. Pa did not whistle about his work as usual, and after a while he said, 'And what we'll do in a wild country without a good watch-dog I don't know.'

3

Camp on the High Prairie

Pa made camp as usual. First, he unhitched and unharnessed Pet and Patty, and he put them on their picket-lines. Picket-lines were long ropes fastened to iron pegs driven into the ground. The pegs were called picket-pins. When horses were on picket-lines they could eat all the grass that the long ropes would let them reach. But when Pet and Patty were put on them, the first thing they did was to lie down and roll back and forth and over. They rolled till the feeling of the harness was all gone from their backs.

While Pet and Patty were rolling, Pa pulled all the grass from a large, round space of ground. There was old, dead grass at the roots of the green grass, and Pa would take no chance of setting the prairie on fire. If fire once started in that dry under-grass, it would sweep the whole country bare and black. Pa said, 'Best be on the safe side, it saves trouble in the end.'

When the space was clear of grass, Pa laid a handful of dry grass in its centre. From the creek bottoms he brought an armful of twigs and dead wood. He laid small twigs and larger twigs and then the wood on the handful of dry grass, and he lighted the grass. The fire crackled merrily inside the ring of bare ground that it couldn't get out of.

Then Pa brought water from the creek, while Mary and

Laura helped Ma get supper. Ma measured coffee beans into the coffee-mill and Mary ground them. Laura filled the coffee-pot with the water Pa brought, and Ma set the pot in the coals. She set the iron bake-oven in the coals, too.

While it heated, she mixed cornmeal and salt with water and patted it into little cakes. She greased the bake-oven with a pork-rind, laid the cornmeal cakes in it, and put on its iron cover. Then Pa raked more coals over the cover, while Ma sliced fat salt pork. She fried the slices in the iron spider. The spider had short legs to stand on in the coals, and that was why it was called a spider. If it had had no legs, it would have been only a frying pan.

The coffee boiled, the cakes baked, the meat fried, and they all smelled so good that Laura grew hungrier and hungrier.

Pa set the wagon-seat near the fire. He and Ma sat on it. Mary and Laura sat on the wagon tongue. Each of them had a tin plate, and a steel knife and a steel fork with white bone handles. Ma had a tin cup and Pa had a tin cup, and Baby Carrie had a little one all her own, but Mary and Laura had to share their tin cup. They drank water. They could not drink coffee until they grew up.

While they were eating supper the purple shadows closed around the camp fire. The vast prairie was dark and still. Only the wind moved stealthily through the grass, and the large, low stars hung glittering from the great sky.

The camp fire was cosy in the big, chill darkness. The slices of pork were crisp and fat, the corncakes were good. In the dark beyond the wagon, Pet and Patty were eating, too. They bit off bites of grass with sharply crunching sounds.

'We'll camp here a day or two,' said Pa. 'Maybe we'll stay here. There's good land, timber in the bottoms, plenty of game—everything a man could want. What do you say, Caroline?'

'We might go farther and fare worse,' Ma replied.

'Anyway, I'll look around tomorrow,' Pa said. 'I'll take my gun and get us some good fresh meat.'

He lighted his pipe with a hot coal, and stretched out his legs comfortably. The warm, brown smell of tobacco smoke mixed with the warmth of the fire. Mary yawned, and slid off the wagon tongue to sit on the grass. Laura yawned, too. Ma quickly washed the tin plates, the tin cups, the knives and forks. She washed the bake-oven and the spider, and rinsed the dish-cloth.

For an instant she was still, listening to the long, wailing howl from the dark prairie. They all knew what it was. But that sound always ran cold up Laura's backbone and crinkled over the back of her head.

Ma shook the dish-cloth, and then she walked into the dark and spread the cloth on the tall grass to dry. When she came back Pa said: 'Wolves. Half a mile away, I'd judge. Well, where there's deer there will be wolves. I wish—'

He didn't say what he wished, but Laura knew. He wished Jack were there. When wolves howled in the Big Woods, Laura had always known that Jack would not let them hurt her. A lump swelled hard in her throat and her nose smarted. She winked fast and did not cry. That wolf, or perhaps another wolf, howled again.

'Bedtime for little girls!' Ma said, cheerfully. Mary got up and turned around so that Ma could unbutton her. But Laura jumped up and stood still. She saw something. Deep in the dark beyond the firelight, two green lights were shining near the ground. They were eyes.

Cold ran up Laura's backbone, her scalp crinkled, her hair stood up. The green lights moved; one winked out, then the other winked out, then both shone steadily, coming nearer. Very rapidly they were coming nearer.

'Look, Pa, look!' Laura said. 'A wolf!'

Pa did not seem to move quickly, but he did. In an instant

he took his gun out of the wagon and was ready to fire at those green eyes. The eyes stopped coming. They were still in the dark, looking at him.

'It can't be a wolf. Unless it's a mad wolf,' Pa said. Ma lifted Mary into the wagon. 'And it's not that,' said Pa. 'Listen to the horses.' Pet and Patty were still biting off bites of grass.

'A lynx?' said Ma.

'Or a coyote?' Pa picked up a stick of wood ; he shouted, and threw it. The green eyes went close to the ground, as if the animal crouched to spring. Pa held the gun ready. The creature did not move.

'Don't, Charles,' Ma said. But Pa slowly walked towards those eyes. And slowly along the ground the eyes crawled towards him. Laura could see the animal in the edge of the dark. It was a tawny animal and brindled. Then Pa shouted and Laura screamed.

The next thing she knew she was trying to hug a jumping, panting, wriggling Jack, who lapped her face and hands with his warm wet tongue. She couldn't hold him. He leaped and wriggled from her to Pa to Ma and back to her again.

'Well, I'm beat!' Pa said.

'So am I,' said Ma. 'But did you have to wake the baby?' She rocked Carrie in her arms, hushing her.

Jack was perfectly well. But soon he lay down close to Laura and sighed a long sigh. His eyes were red with tiredness, and all the under part of him was caked with mud. Ma gave him a cornmeal cake and he licked it and wagged politely, but he could not eat. He was too tired.

'No telling how long he kept swimming,' Pa said. 'Nor how far he was carried downstream before he landed.' And when at last he reached them, Laura called him a wolf, and Pa threatened to shoot him.

But Jack knew they didn't mean it. Laura asked him, 'You knew we didn't mean it, didn't you, Jack?' Jack wagged his stump of a tail; he knew.

It was past bedtime. Pa chained Pet and Patty to the feed-box at the back of the wagon and fed them their corn. Carrie slept again, and Ma helped Mary and Laura undress. She put their long nightgowns over their heads while they stuck their arms into the sleeves. They buttoned the neckbands themselves, and tied the strings of their nightcaps beneath their chins. Under the wagon Jack wearily turned around three times, and lay down to sleep.

In the wagon Laura and Mary said their prayers and crawled into their little bed. Ma kissed them good night.

On the other side of the canvas, Pet and Patty were eating their corn. When Patty whooshed into the feed-box, the whoosh was right at Laura's ear. There were little scurrying sounds in the grass. In the trees by the creek an owl called, 'Who-oo? who-oo?' Farther away another owl answered, 'Oo-oo, oo-oo.' Far away on the prairie the wolves howled, and under the wagon Jack growled low in his chest. In the wagon everything was safe and snug.

Thickly in front of the open wagon-top hung the large, glittering stars. Pa could reach them, Laura thought. She wished he would pick the largest one from the thread on which it hung from the sky, and give it to her. She was wide awake, she was not sleepy at all, but suddenly she was very much surprised. The large star winked at her!

Then she was waking up, next morning.

4

Prairie Day

Soft whickerings were close to Laura's ear, and grain rattled into the feed-box. Pa was giving Pet and Patty their breakfasts.

'Back, Pet! Don't be greedy,' he said. 'You know it's Patty's turn.'

Pet stamped her foot and nickered.

'Now, Patty, keep your own end of the box,' said Pa. 'This is for Pet.'

Then a little squeal from Patty.

'Hah! Got nipped, didn't you?' Pa said. 'And serve you right. I told you to eat your own corn.'

Mary and Laura looked at each other and laughed. They could smell bacon and coffee and hear pancakes sizzling, and they scrambled out of bed.

Mary could dress herself, all but the middle button. Laura buttoned that one for her, then Mary buttoned Laura all the way up the back. They washed their hands and faces in the tin wash-basin on the wagon-step. Ma combed every tangle out of their hair, while Pa brought fresh water from the creek.

Then they sat on the clean grass and ate pancakes and bacon and molasses from the tin plates in their laps.

All around them shadows were moving over the waving grasses, while the sun rose. Meadow larks were springing straight up from the billows of grass into the high, clear sky, singing as they went. Small pearly clouds drifted in the immense blueness overhead. In all the weed-tops tiny birds were swinging and singing in tiny voices. Pa said they were dickcissels.

'Dickie, dickie!' Laura called back to them. 'Dickie bird!'

'Eat your breakfast, Laura,' Ma said. 'You must mind your manners, even if we are a hundred miles from anywhere.'

Pa said, mildly, 'It's only forty miles to Independence, Caroline, and no doubt there's a neighbour or so nearer than that.'

'Forty miles, then,' Ma agreed. 'But whether or not, it isn't good manners to sing at table. Or when you're eating,' she added, because there was no table.

There was only the enormous, empty prairie, with grasses blowing in waves of light and shadow across it, and the great blue sky above it, and birds flying up from it and singing with joy because the sun was rising. And on the whole enormous prairie there was no sign that any other human being had ever been there.

In all that space of land and sky stood the lonely, small, covered wagon. And close to it sat Pa and Ma and Laura and Mary and Baby Carrie, eating their breakfasts. The mustangs munched their corn, and Jack sat still, trying hard not to beg. Laura was not allowed to feed him while she ate, but she saved bits for him. And Ma made a big pancake for him, of the last of the batter.

Rabbits were everywhere in the grass, and thousands of prairie chickens, but Jack could not hunt his breakfast that day. Pa was going hunting, and Jack must guard the camp.

First Pa put Pet and Patty on their picket-lines. Then he took the wooden tub from the side of the wagon and filled it with water from the creek. Ma was going to do the washing.

Then Pa stuck his sharp hatchet in his belt, he hung his powder-horn beside the hatchet, he put the patch-box and the bullet-pouch in his pocket, and he took his gun on his arm.

He said to Ma: 'Take your time, Caroline. We won't move the wagon till we want to. We've got all the time there is.'

He went away. For a little while they could see the upper part of him above the tall grasses, going away and growing smaller. Then he went out of sight and the prairie was empty.

Mary and Laura washed the dishes while Ma made the beds in the wagon. They put the clean dishes neatly in their box; they picked up every scattered twig and put it in the fire; they stacked the wood against a wagon wheel. Then everything about the camp was tidy.

Ma brought the wooden pannikin of soft soap from the wagon. She kilted up her skirts and rolled up her sleeves, and she knelt by the tub on the grass. She washed sheets and pillow-cases and white underthings, she washed dresses and shirts, and she rinsed them in clear water and spread them on the clean grass, to dry in the sun.

Mary and Laura were exploring. They must not go far from the wagon, but it was fun to run through the tall grass, in the sunshine and wind. Huge rabbits bounded away before them, birds fluttered up and settled again. The tiny dickie-birds were everywhere, and their tiny nests were in the tall weeds. And everywhere were little brown-striped gophers.

These little creatures looked soft as velvet. They had bright round eyes and crinkling noses and wee paws. They popped out of holes in the ground, and stood up to look at Mary and Laura. Their hind legs folded under their haunches, their little paws folded tight to their chests, and they looked exactly like bits of dead wood sticking out of the ground. Only their bright eyes glittered.

Mary and Laura wanted to catch one to take to Ma. Again

and again they almost had one. The gopher would stand perfectly still until you were sure you had him this time, then just as you touched him, he wasn't there. There was only his round hole in the ground.

Laura ran and ran, and couldn't catch one. Mary sat perfectly still beside a hole, waiting for one to come up, and just beyond her reach gophers scampered merrily, and gophers sat up and looked at her. But not one ever came out of that hole.

Once a shadow floated across the grass, and every gopher vanished. A hawk was sailing overhead. It was so close that Laura saw its cruel round eye turned downward to look at her. She saw its sharp beak and its savage claws curled ready to pounce. But the hawk saw nothing but Laura and Mary and round, empty holes in the ground. It sailed away, looking somewhere else for its dinner.

Then all the little gophers came up again.

It was nearly noon then. The sun was almost overhead. So Laura and Mary picked flowers from the weeds, and they took the flowers to Ma, instead of a gopher.

Ma was folding the dry clothes. The little panties and petticoats were whiter than snow, warm from the sun, and smelling like the grass. Ma laid them in the wagon, and took the flowers. She admired equally the flowers that Laura gave her and the flowers that Mary gave her, and she put them together in a tin cup full of water. She set them on the wagon-step, to make the camp pretty.

Then she split two cold corn-cakes and spread them with molasses. She gave one to Mary and one to Laura. That was their dinner, and it was very good.

'Where is a papoose, Ma?' Laura asked.

'Don't speak with your mouth full, Laura,' said Ma.

So Laura chewed and swallowed, and she said, 'I want to see a papoose.'

'Mercy on us!' Ma said. 'Whatever makes you want to

see Indians? We will see enough of them. More than we want to, I wouldn't wonder.'

'They wouldn't hurt us, would they?' Mary asked. Mary was always good; she never spoke with her mouth full.

'No!' Ma said. 'Don't get such an idea into your head.'

'Why don't you like Indians, Ma?' Laura asked, and she caught a drip of molasses with her tongue.

'I just don't like them; and don't lick your fingers, Laura,' said Ma.

'This is Indian country, isn't it?' Laura said. 'What did we come to their country for, if you don't like them?'

Ma said she didn't know whether this was Indian country or not. She didn't know where the Kansas line was. But whether or no, the Indians would not be here long. Pa had word from a man in Washington that the Indian Territory would be open to settlement soon. It might already be open to settlement. They could not know, because Washington was so far away.

Then Ma took the flat-iron out of the wagon and heated it by the fire. She sprinkled a dress for Mary and a dress for Laura and a little dress for Baby Carrie, and her own sprigged calico. She spread a blanket and a sheet on the wagon seat, and she ironed the dresses.

Baby Carrie slept in the wagon. Laura and Mary and Jack lay on the shady grass beside it, because now the sunshine was hot. Jack's mouth was open and his red tongue hung out, his eyes blinked sleepily. Ma hummed softly to herself while the iron smoothed all the wrinkles out of the little dresses. All around them, to the very edge of the world, there was nothing but grasses waving in the wind. Far overhead, a few white puffs of cloud sailed in the thin blue air.

Laura was very happy. The wind sang a low, rustling song in the grass. Grasshoppers' rasping quivered up from all the immense prairie. A buzzing came faintly from all the trees in the creek bottoms. But all these sounds made a great, warm, happy silence. Laura had never seen a place she liked so much as this place.

She didn't know she had gone to sleep until she woke up. Jack was on his feet, wagging his stump tail. The sun was low, and Pa was coming across the prairie. Laura jumped up and ran, and his long shadow stretched to meet her in the waving grasses.

He held up the game in his hand, for her to see. He had a rabbit, the largest rabbit she had ever seen, and two plump prairie hens. Laura jumped up and down and clapped her hands and squealed. Then she caught hold of his other sleeve and hippety-hopped through the tall grasses beside him.

'This country's cram-jammed with game,' he told her. 'I saw fifty deer if I saw one, and antelope, squirrels, rabbits, birds of all kinds. The creek's full of fish.' He said to Ma, 'I tell you, Caroline, there's everything we want here. We can live like kings!'

That was a wonderful supper. They sat by the camp fire and ate the tender, savoury, flavoury meat till they could eat no more. When at last Laura set down her plate, she sighed with contentment. She didn't want anything more in the world.

The last colour was fading from the enormous sky and all the level land was shadowy. The warmth of the fire was pleasant because the night wind was cool. Phoebebirds called sadly from the woods down by the creek. For a little while a mocking-bird sang, then the stars came out and the birds were still.

Softly Pa's fiddle sang in the starlight. Sometimes he sang a little and sometimes the fiddle sang alone. Sweet and thin and far away, the fiddle went on singing

'None knew thee but to love thee,
Thou dear one of my heart …'

The large, bright stars hung down from the sky. Lower and lower they came, quivering with music.

Laura gasped, and Ma came quickly. 'What is it, Laura?' she asked, and Laura whispered, 'The stars were singing.'

'You've been asleep,' Ma said. 'It is only the fiddle. And it's time little girls were in bed.'

She undressed Laura in the firelight and put her nightgown on and tied her nightcap, and tucked her into bed. But the fiddle was still singing in the starlight. The night was full of music, and Laura was sure that part of it came from the great, bright stars swinging so low above the prairie.

5

The House on the Prairie

Laura and Mary were up next morning earlier than the sun. They ate their breakfast of cornmeal mush with prairie-hen gravy, and hurried to help Ma wash the dishes. Pa was loading everything else into the wagon and hitching up Pet and Patty.

When the sun rose, they were driving on across the prairie. There was no road now. Pet and Patty waded through the grasses, and the wagon left behind it only the tracks of its wheels.

Before noon, Pa said, 'Whoa!' The wagon stopped.

'Here we are, Caroline!' he said. 'Right here we'll build our house.'

Laura and Mary scrambled over the feed-box and dropped to the ground in a hurry. All around them there was nothing but grassy prairie spreading to the edge of the sky.

Quite near them, to the north, the creek bottoms lay below the prairie. Some darker green tree-tops showed, and beyond them bits of the rim of earthen bluffs held up the prairie's grasses. Far away to the east, a broken line of different greens lay on the prairie, and Pa said that was the river.

'That's the Verdigris River,' he said, pointing it out to Ma.

Right away, he and Ma began to unload the wagon. They took out everything and piled it on the ground.

Then they took off the wagon-cover and put it over the pile. Then they took even the wagon-box off, while Laura and Mary and Jack watched.

The wagon had been home for a long time. Now there was nothing left of it but the four wheels and the parts that connected them. Pet and Patty were still hitched to the tongue. Pa took a bucket and his axe, and sitting on this skeleton wagon, he drove away. He drove right down into the prairie, out of sight.

'Where's Pa going?' Laura asked, and Ma said, 'He's going to get a load of logs from the creek bottoms.'

It was strange and frightening to be left without the wagon on the High Prairie. The land and the sky seemed too large, and Laura felt small. She wanted to hide and be still in the tall grass, like a little prairie chicken. But she didn't. She helped Ma, while Mary sat on the grass and minded Baby Carrie.

First Laura and Ma made the beds, under the wagon-cover tent. Then Ma arranged the boxes and bundles, while Laura pulled all the grass from a space in front of the tent. That made a bare place for the fire. They couldn't start the fire until Pa brought wood.

There was nothing more to do, so Laura explored a little. She did not go far from the tent. But she found a queer little kind of tunnel in the grass. You'd never notice it if you looked across the waving grass-tops. But when you came to it, there it was—a narrow, straight, hard path down between the grass stems. It went out into the endless prairie.

Laura went along it a little way. She went slowly, and more slowly, and then she stood still and felt queer. So she turned around and came back quickly. When she looked over her shoulder there wasn't anything there. But she hurried.

When Pa came riding back on a load of logs, Laura told him about that path. He said he had seen it yesterday. 'It's some old trail,' he said.

That night by the fire Laura asked again when she would see a papoose, but Pa didn't know. He said you never saw Indians unless they wanted you to see them. He had seen Indians when he was a boy in New York State, but Laura never had. She knew they were wild men with red skins, and their hatchets were called tomahawks.

Pa knew all about wild animals, so he must know about wild men, too. Laura thought he would show her a papoose some day, just as he had shown her lawns, and little bears, and wolves.

For days Pa hauled logs. He made two piles of them, one for the house and one for the stable. There began to be a road where he drove back and forth to the creek bottoms. And at night on their picket-lines Pet and Patty ate the grass, till it was short and stubby all around the log-piles.

Pa began the house first. He paced off the size of it on the ground, then with his spade he dug a shallow little hollow along two sides of that space. Into these hollows he rolled two of the biggest logs. They were sound, strong logs, because they must hold up the house. They were called sills.

Then Pa chose two more strong, big logs, and he rolled these logs on to the ends of the sills, so that they made a hollow square. Now with his axe he cut a wide, deep notch near each end of these logs. He cut these notches out of the top of the log, but with his eye he measured the sills, and he cut the notches so that they would fit around half of the sill.

When the notches were cut, he rolled the log over. And the notches fitted down over the sill.

That finished the foundation of the house. It was one log high. The sills were half buried in the ground, and the logs on their ends fitted snugly to the ground. At the corners, where they crossed, the notches let them fit together so that they were no thicker than one log. And the two ends stuck out beyond the notches.

Next day Pa began the walls. From each side he rolled up a log, and he notched its ends so that it fitted down over the end logs. Then he rolled up logs from the ends, and notched them so that they fitted down over the side logs. Now the whole house was two logs high.

The logs fitted solidly together at the corners. But no log is ever perfectly straight, and all logs are bigger at one end than at the other end, so cracks were left between them all along the walls. But that did not matter, because Pa would chink those cracks.

All by himself, he built the house three logs high. Then Ma helped him. Pa lifted one end of a log on to the wall, then Ma held it while he lifted the other end. He stood up on the wall to cut the notches, and Ma helped roll and hold the log while he settled it where it should be to make the corner perfectly square.

So, log by log, they built the walls higher, till they were pretty high, and Laura couldn't get over them any more. She was tired of watching Pa and Ma build the house, and she went into the tall grass, exploring. Suddenly she heard Pa shout, 'Let go! Get out from under!'

The big, heavy log was sliding. Pa was trying to hold up his end of it, to keep it from falling on Ma. He couldn't. It crashed down. Laura saw Ma huddled on the ground.

She got to Ma almost as quickly as Pa did. Pa knelt down and called Ma in a dreadful voice, and Ma gasped, 'I'm all right.'

The log was on her foot. Pa lifted the log and Ma pulled her foot from under it, Pa felt her to see if any bones were broken.

'Move your arms,' he said. 'Is your back hurt? Can you turn your head?' Ma moved her arms and turned her head.

'Thank God,' Pa said. He helped Ma to sit up. She said again, 'I'm all right, Charles. It's just my foot.'

Quickly Pa took off her shoe and stocking. He felt her foot all over, moving the ankle and the instep and every toe. 'Does it hurt much?' he asked.

Ma's face was grey and her mouth was a tight line. 'Not much,' she said.

'No bones broken,' said Pa. 'It's only a bad sprain.'

Ma said cheerfully: 'Well, a sprain's soon mended. Don't be so upset, Charles.'

'I blame myself,' said Pa. 'I should have used skids.'

He helped Ma to the tent. He built up the fire and heated water. When the water was as hot as Ma could bear, she put her swollen foot into it.

It was providential that the foot was not crushed. Only a little hollow in the ground had saved it.

Pa kept pouring more hot water into the tub in which Ma's foot was soaking. Her foot was red from the heat and the puffed ankle began to turn purple. Ma took her foot out of the water and bound strips of rag tightly round and round the ankle. 'I can manage,' she said.

She could not get her shoe on. But she tied more rags around her foot, and she hobbled on it. She got supper as usual, only a little more slowly. But Pa said she could not help to build the house until her ankle was well.

He hewed out skids. These were long, flat slabs. One end rested on the ground, and the other end rested on the log wall. He was not going to lift any more logs; he and Ma would roll them up these skids.

But Ma's ankle was not well yet. When she unwrapped it in the evenings, to soak it in hot water, it was all purple and black and green and yellow. The house must wait.

Then one afternoon Pa came merrily whistling up the creek road. They had not expected him home from hunting so soon. As soon as he saw them he shouted, 'Good news!'

They had a neighbour, only two miles away on the other side of the creek. Pa had met him in the woods. They were going to trade work and that would make it easier for everyone.

'He's a bachelor,' said Pa, 'and he says he can get along without a house better than you and the girls can. So he's going to help me first. Then as soon as he gets his logs ready, I'll go over and help him.'

They need not wait any longer for the house, and Ma need not do any more work on it.

'How do you like that, Caroline?' Pa asked, joyfully; and Ma said, 'That's good, Charles. I'm glad.'

Early next morning Mr Edwards came. He was lean and tall and brown. He bowed to Ma and called her 'Ma'am' politely. But he told Laura that he was a wild-cat from Tennessee. He wore tall boots and a ragged jumper, and a coonskin cap, and he could spit tobacco juice farther than Laura had ever imagined that anyone could spit tobacco juice. He could hit anything he spat at, too. Laura tried and tried, but she could never spit so far or so well as Mr Edwards could.

He was a fast worker. In one day he and Pa built those walls as high as Pa wanted them. They joked and sang while they worked, and their axes made the chips fly.

On top of the walls they set up a skeleton roof of slender poles. Then in the south wall they cut a tall hole for a door, and in the west wall and the east wall they cut square holes for windows.

Laura couldn't wait to see the inside of the house. As soon as the tall hole was cut, she ran inside. Everything was striped there. Stripes of sunshine came through the cracks in the west wall, and stripes of shadow came down from the poles overhead. The stripes of shade and sunshine were all across Laura's hands and her arms and her bare feet. And through the cracks between the logs she could see stripes of prairie.

The sweet smell of the prairie mixed with the sweet smell of cut wood.

Then, as Pa cut away the logs to make the window hole in the west wall, chunks of sunshine came in. When he finished, a big block of sunshine lay on the ground inside the house.

Around the door hole and the window holes Pa and Mr Edwards nailed thin slabs against the cut ends of the logs. And the house was finished, all but the roof. The walls were solid and the house was large, much larger than the tent. It was a nice house.

Mr Edwards said he would go home now, but Pa and Ma said he must stay to supper. Ma had cooked an especially good supper because they had company.

There was stewed jack rabbit with white-flour dumplings and plenty of gravy. There was a steaming hot, thick cornbread flavoured with bacon fat. There was molasses to eat on the cornbread, but because this was a company supper they did not sweeten their coffee with molasses. Ma brought out the little paper sack of pale brown store sugar.

Mr Edwards said he surely did appreciate that supper.

Then Pa brought out his fiddle.

Mr Edwards stretched out on the ground, to listen. But first Pa played for Laura and Mary. He played their very favourite song, and he sang it. Laura liked it best of all because Pa's voice went down deep, deep, deeper in that song.

> 'Oh, I am a Gipsy King!
> I come and go as I please!
> I pull my old nightcap down,
> And take the world at my ease.'

Then his voice went deep, deep down, deeper than the very oldest bullfrog's.

'Oh!

I am

a

Gyp-

sy

KING!'

They all laughed. Laura could hardly stop laughing.

'Oh, sing it again, Pa! Sing it again!' she cried, before she remembered that children must be seen and not heard. Then she was quiet.

Pa went on playing, and everything began to dance. Mr Edwards rose up on one elbow, then he sat up, then he jumped up and he danced. He danced like a jumpingjack in the moonlight, while Pa's fiddle kept on rollicking and his foot kept tapping the ground, and Laura's hands and Mary's hands were clapping together and their feet were patting, too.

'You're the fiddlin'est fool that ever I see!' Mr Edwards shouted admiringly to Pa. He didn't stop dancing, Pa didn't stop playing. He played 'Money Musk' and 'Arkansas Traveller', 'Irish Washerwoman' and the 'Devil's Hornpipe'.

Baby Carrie couldn't sleep in all that music. She sat up in Ma's lap, looking at Mr Edwards with round eyes, and clapping her little hands and laughing.

Even the firelight danced, and all around its edge the shadows were dancing. Only the new house stood still and quiet in the dark, till the big moon rose and shone on its grey walls and the yellow chips around it.

Mr Edwards said he must go. It was a long way back to his camp on the other side of the woods and the creek. He took his gun, and said good night to Laura and Mary and Ma. He said a bachelor got mighty lonesome, and he surely had enjoyed this evening of home life.

'Play, Ingalls!' he said. 'Play me down the road!' So while

he went down the creek road and out of sight, Pa played, and Pa and Mr Edwards and Laura sang with all their might.

> 'Old Dan Tucker was a fine old man;
> He washed his face in the frying-pan,
> He combed his hair with a wagon wheel,
> And died of the toothache in his heel.
>
> 'Git out of the way for old Dan Tucker!
> He's too late to get his supper!
> Supper's over and the dishes washed,
> Nothing left but a piece of squash!
>
> 'Old Dan Tucker went to town,
> Riding a mule, leading a houn'…'

Far over the prairie rang Pa's big voice and Laura's little one, and faintly from the creek bottoms came a last whoop from Mr Edwards.

> 'Git out of the way for old Dan Tucker!
> He's too late to get his supper!'

When Pa's fiddle stopped, they could not hear Mr Edwards any more. Only the wind rustled in the prairie grasses. The big, yellow moon was sailing high overhead. The sky was so full of light that not one star twinkled in it, and all the prairie was a shadowy mellowness.

Then from the woods by the creek a nightingale began to sing.

Everything was silent, listening to the nightingale's song. The bird sang on and on. The cool wind moved over the prairie and the song was round and clear above the grasses' whispering. The sky was like a bowl of light overturned on the flat black land.

The song ended. No one moved or spoke. Laura and Mary were quiet, Pa and Ma sat motionless. Only the wind stirred and the grasses sighed. Then Pa lifted the fiddle to his shoulder and softly touched the bow to the strings. A few notes fell like clear drops of water into the stillness. A pause, and Pa began to play the nightingale's song. The nightingale answered him. The nightingale began to sing again. It was singing with Pa's fiddle.

When the strings were silent, the nightingale went on singing. When it paused, the fiddle called to it and it sang again. The bird and the fiddle were talking to each other in the cool night under the moon.

6

Moving In

'The walls are up,' Pa was saying to Main the morning. 'We'd better move in and get along as best we can without a floor or other fixings. I must build the stable as fast as I can, so Pet and Patty can be inside walls, too. Last night I could hear wolves howling from every direction, seemed like, and close, too.'

'Well, you have your gun, so I'll not worry,' said Ma.

'Yes, and there's Jack. But I'll feel easier in my mind when you and the girls have good solid walls around you.'

'Why do you suppose we haven't seen any Indians?' Ma asked.

'Oh, I don't know,' Pa replied, carelessly. 'I've seen their camping-places among the bluffs. They're away on a hunting-trip now, I guess.'

Then Ma called: 'Girls! The sun's up!' and Laura and Mary scrambled out of bed and into their clothes.

'Eat your breakfasts quickly,' Ma said, putting the last of the rabbit stew on their tin plates. 'We're moving into the house today, and all the chips must be out.'

So they ate quickly, and hurried to carry all the chips out of the house. They ran back and forth as fast as they could, gathering their skirts full of chips and dumping them in a pile near the fire. But there were still chips on the ground inside the house when Ma began to sweep it with her willow-bough broom.

Ma limped, though her sprained ankle was beginning to get well. But she soon swept the earthen floor, and then Mary and Laura began to help her carry things into the house.

Pa was on top of the walls, stretching the canvas wagontop over the skeleton roof of saplings. The canvas billowed in the wind, Pa's beard blew wildly and his hair stood up from his head as if it were trying to pull itself out. He held on to the canvas and fought it. Once it jerked so hard that Laura thought he must let go or sail into the air like a bird. But he held tight to the wall with his legs, and tight to the canvas with his hands, and he tied it down.

'There!' he said to it. 'Stay where you are, and be—'

'Charles!' Ma said. She stood with her arms full of quilts and looked up at him reprovingly.

'—and be good,' Pa said to the canvas. 'Why, Caroline, what did you think I was going to say?'

'Oh, Charles!' Ma said. 'You scallawag!'

Pa came right down the corner of the house. The ends of the logs stuck out, and he used them for a ladder. He ran his hand through his hair so that it stood up even more wildly, and Ma burst out laughing. Then he hugged her, quilts and all.

Then they looked at the house and Pa said, 'How's that for a snug house!'

'I'll be thankful to get into it,' said Ma.

There was no door and there were no windows. There was no floor except the ground and no roof except the canvas. But that house had good stout walls, and it would stay where it was. It was not like the wagon, that every morning went on to some other place.

'We're going to do well here, Caroline,' Pa said. 'This is a great country. This is a country I'll be contented to stay in the rest of my life.'

'Even when it's settled up?' Ma asked.

'Even when it's settled up. No matter how thick and close the neighbours get, this country'll never feel crowded. Look at that sky!'

Laura knew what he meant. She liked this place, too. She liked the enormous sky and the winds, and the land that you couldn't see to the end of. Everything was so fresh and clean and big and splendid.

By dinner-time the house was in order. The beds were neatly made on the floor. The wagon-seat and two ends of logs were brought in for chairs. Pa's gun lay on its pegs above the doorway. Boxes and bundles were neat against the walls. It was a pleasant house. A soft light came through the canvas roof, wind and sunshine came through the window holes, and every crack in the four walls glowed a little because the sun was overhead.

Only the camp fire stayed where it had been. Pa said he would build a fireplace in the house as soon as he could. He would hew out slabs to make a solid roof, too, before winter came. He would lay a puncheon floor, and make beds and tables and chairs. But all that work must wait until he had helped Mr Edwards and had built a stable for Pet and Patty.

'When that's all done,' said Ma, 'I want a clothes-line.'

Pa laughed. 'Yes, and I want a well.'

After dinner he hitched Pet and Patty to the wagon and he hauled a tubful of water from the creek, so that Ma could do the washing. 'You could wash clothes in the creek,' he told her. 'Indian women do.'

'If we wanted to live like Indians, you could make a hole in the roof to let the smoke out, and we'd have the fire on the floor inside the house,' said Ma. 'Indians do.'

That afternoon she washed the clothes in the tub and spread them on the grass to dry.

After supper they sat for a while by the camp fire. That night they would sleep in the house; they would never sleep beside a campfire again. Pa and Ma talked about the folks in

Wisconsin, and Ma wished she could send them a letter. But Independence was forty miles away, and no letter could go until Pa made the long trip to the post-office there.

Back in the Big Woods so far away, Grandpa and Grandma and the aunts and uncles and cousins did not know where Pa and Ma and Laura and Mary and Baby Carrie were. And sitting there by the camp fire, no one knew what might have happened in the Big Woods. There was no way to find out.

'Well, it's bedtime,' Ma said. Baby Carrie was already asleep. Ma carried her into the house and undressed her, while Mary unbuttoned Laura's dress and petticoat waist down the back, and Pa hung a quilt over the door hole. The quilt would be better than no door. Then Pa went out to bring Pet and Patty close to the house.

He called back, softly, 'Come out here, Caroline, and look at the moon.'

Mary and Laura lay in their little bed on the ground inside the new house, and watched the sky through the window hole to the east. The edge of the big, bright moon glittered at the bottom of the window space, and Laura sat up. She looked at the great moon, sailing silently higher in the clear sky.

Its light made silvery lines in all the cracks on that side of the house. The light poured through the window hole and made a square of soft radiance on the floor. It was so bright that Laura saw Ma plainly when she lifted the quilt at the door and came in.

Then Laura very quickly lay down, before Ma saw her naughtily sitting up in bed.

She heard Pet and Patty whinnying softly to Pa. Then the faint thuds of their feet came into her ear from the floor. Pet and Patty and Pa were coming towards the house, and Laura heard Pa singing:

'Sail on, silver moon!
Shed your radiance o'er the sky—'

His voice was like a part of the night and the moonlight and the stillness of the prairie. He came to the doorway, singing,

'By the pale, silver light of the moon—'

Softly Ma said, 'Hush, Charles. You'll wake the children.'

So Pa came in without a sound. Jack followed at his heels and lay down across the doorway. Now they were all inside the stout walls of their new home, and they were snug and safe. Drowsily Laura heard a long wolf-howl rising from far away on the prairie, but only a little shiver went up her backbone and she fell asleep.

7

The Wolf-Pack

All in one day Pa and Mr Edwards built the stable for Pet and Patty. They even put the roof on, working so late that Ma had to keep supper waiting for them.

There was no stable door, but in the moonlight Pa drove two stout posts well into the ground, one on either side of the doorway. He put Pet and Patty inside the stable, and then he laid small, split logs one above another, across the door space. The posts held them, and they made a solid wall.

'Now!' said Pa. 'Let those wolves howl! I'll sleep, tonight.'

In the morning, when he lifted the split logs from behind the posts, Laura was amazed. Beside Pet stood a longlegged, long-eared, wobbly little colt.

When Laura ran towards it, gentle Pet laid back her ears and snapped her teeth at Laura.

'Keep back, Laura!' Pa said, sharply. He said to Pet, 'Now, Pet, you know we won't hurt your little colt.' Pet answered him with a soft whinny. She would let Pa stroke her colt, but she would not let Laura or Mary come near it. When they even peeked at it through the cracks in the stable wall, Pet rolled the whites of her eyes at them and showed them her teeth. They had never seen a colt with ears so long. Pa said it was a little mule, but Laura said it looked like a jack rabbit. So they named the little colt Bunny.

When Pet was on the picket-line, with Bunny frisking around her and wondering at the big world, Laura must watch Baby Carrie carefully. If anyone but Pa came near Bunny, Pet squealed with rage and dashed to bite that little girl.

Early that Sunday afternoon Pa rode Patty away across the prairie to see what he should see. There was plenty of meat in the house, so he did not take his gun.

He rode away through the tall grass, along the rim of the creek bluffs. Birds flew up before him and circled and sank into the grasses. Pa was looking down into the creek bottoms as he rode; perhaps he was watching deer browsing there. Then Patty broke into a gallop, and swiftly she and Pa grew smaller. Soon there was only waving grass where they had been.

Late that afternoon Pa had not come home. Ma stirred the coals of the fire and laid chips on them, and began to get supper. Mary was in the house, minding the baby, and Laura asked Ma, 'What's the matter with Jack?'

Jack was walking up and down, looking worried. He wrinkled his nose at the wind, and the hair rose up on his neck and lay down, and then rose up again. Pet's hoofs suddenly thudded. She ran around the circle of her picket-rope and stood still, whickering a low whicker. Bunny came close to her.

'What's the matter, Jack?' Ma asked. He looked up at her, but he couldn't say anything. Ma gazed around the whole circle of earth and sky. She could not see anything unusual.

'Likely it isn't anything, Laura,' she said. She raked coals around the coffee-pot and the spider and on to the top of the bake-oven. The prairie hen sizzled in the spider and the corncakes began to smell good. But all the time Ma kept glancing at the prairie all around. Jack walked about restlessly, and Pet did not graze. She faced the north-west, where Pa had gone, and kept her colt close beside her.

All at once Patty came running across the prairie. She was stretched out, running with all her might, and Pa was leaning almost flat on her neck.

She ran right past the stable before Pa could stop her. He stopped her so hard that she almost sat down. She was trembling all over and her black coat was streaked with sweat and foam. Pa swung off her. He was breathing hard, too.

'What is the matter, Charles?' Ma asked him.

Pa was looking towards the creek, so Ma and Laura looked at it, too. But they could see only the space above the bottom lands, with a few tree-tops in it, and the distant tops of the earthen bluffs under the High Prairie's grasses.

'What is it?' Ma asked again. 'Why did you ride Patty like that?'

Pa breathed a long breath. 'I was afraid the wolves would beat me here. But I see everything's all right.'

'Wolves!' she cried. 'What wolves?'

'Everything's all right, Caroline,' said Pa. 'Let a fellow get his breath.'

When he had got some breath, he said, 'I didn't ride Patty like that. It was all I could do to hold her at all. Fifty wolves, Caroline, the biggest wolves I ever saw. I wouldn't go through such a thing again, not for a mint of money.'

A shadow came over the prairie just then because the sun had gone down, and Pa said, 'I'll tell you about it later.'

'We'll eat supper in the house,' said Ma.

'No need of that,' he told her. 'Jack will give us warning in plenty of time.'

He brought Pet and her colt from the picket-line. He didn't take them and Patty to drink from the creek, as he usually did. He gave them the water in Ma's washtub, which was standing full, ready for the washing next morning. He rubbed down Patty's sweaty sides and legs and put her in the barn with Pet and Bunny.

Supper was ready. The camp fire made a circle of light in

the dark. Laura and Mary stayed close to the fire, and kept Baby Carrie with them. They could feel the dark all around them, and they kept looking behind them at the place where the dark mixed with the edge of the firelight. Shadows moved there, as if they were alive.

Jack sat on his haunches beside Laura. The edges of his ears were lifted, listening to the dark. Now and then he walked a little way into it. He walked all around the camp fire, and came back to sit beside Laura. The hair lay flat on his thick neck and he did not growl. His teeth showed a little, but that was because he was a bulldog.

Laura and Mary ate their corncakes and the prairie hen's drumsticks, and they listened to Pa while he told Ma about the wolves.

He had found some more neighbours. Settlers were coming in and settling along both sides of the creek. Less than three miles away, in a hollow on the High Prairie, a man and his wife were building a house. Their name was Scott, and Pa said they were nice folks. Six miles beyond them, two bachelors were living in one house. They had taken two farms, and built the house on the line between them. One man's bunk was against one wall of the house, and the other man's bunk was against the other wall. So each man slept on his own farm, although they were in the same house and the house was only eight feet wide. They cooked and ate together in the middle of the house.

Pa had not said anything about the wolves yet. Laura wished he would. But she knew that she must not interrupt when Pa was talking.

He said that these bachelors did not know that anyone else was in the country. They had seen nobody but Indians. So they were glad to see Pa, and he stayed there longer than he had meant to.

Then he rode on, and from a little rise in the prairie he saw a white speck down in the creek bottoms. He thought it was a covered wagon, and it was. When he came to it, he found a man and his wife and five children. They had come from Iowa, and they had camped in the bottoms because one of their horses was sick. The horse was better now, but the bad night air so near the creek had given them fever 'n' ague. The man and his wife and the three oldest children were too sick to stand up. The little boy and girl, no bigger than Mary and Laura, were taking care of them.

So Pa did what he could for them, and then he rode back to tell the bachelors about them. One of them rode right away to fetch that family up on the High Prairie, where they would soon get well in the good air.

One thing had led to another, until Pa was starting home later than he had meant. He took a short cut across the prairie, and as he was loping along on Patty, suddenly out of a little draw came a pack of wolves. They were all around Pa in a moment.

'It was a big pack,' Pa said. 'All of fifty wolves, and the biggest wolves I ever saw in my life. Must be what they call buffalo wolves. Their leader's a big grey brute that stands three feet at the shoulder, if an inch. I tell you my hair stood straight on end.'

'And you didn't have your gun,' said Ma.

'I thought of that. But my gun would have been no use if I'd had it. You can't fight fifty wolves with one gun. And Patty couldn't outrun them.'

'What did you do?' Ma asked.

'Nothing,' said Pa. 'Patty tried to run. I never wanted anything worse than I wanted to get away from there. But I knew if Patty even started, those wolves would be on us in a minute, pulling us down. So I held Patty to a walk.'

'Goodness, Charles!' Ma said under her breath.

'Yes. I wouldn't go through such a thing again for any money. Caroline, I never saw such wolves. One big fellow trotted along, right by my stirrup. I could have kicked him in the ribs. They didn't pay any attention to me at all. They must have just made a kill and eaten all they could.

'I tell you, Caroline, those wolves just closed in around Patty and me and trotted along with us. In broad daylight. For all the world like a pack of dogs going along with a horse. They were all around us, trotting along, and jumping and playing and snapping at each other, just like dogs.'

'Goodness, Charles!' Ma said again. Laura's heart was thumping fast, and her mouth and her eyes were wide open, staring at Pa.

'Patty was shaking all over, and fighting the bit,' said Pa. 'Sweat ran off her, she was so scared. I was sweating, too. But I held her down to a walk, and we went walking along among those wolves. They came right along with us, a quarter of a mile or more. That big fellow trotted by my stirrup as if he were there to stay.

'Then we came to the head of a draw, running down into the creek bottoms. The big grey leader went down it, and all the rest of the pack trotted down into it, behind him. As soon as the last one was in the draw, I let Patty go.

'She headed straight for home, across the prairie. And she couldn't have run faster if I'd been cutting into her with a rawhide whip. I was scared the whole way. I thought the wolves might be coming this way and they might be making better time than I was. I was glad you had the gun, Caroline. And glad the house is built. I knew you could keep the wolves out of the house, with the gun. But Pet and the colt were outside.'

'You need not have worried, Charles,' Ma said. 'I guess I would manage to save our horses.'

'I was not fully reasonable, at the time,' said Pa. 'I know you would save the horses, Caroline. Those wolves wouldn't bother you, anyway. If they had been hungry, I wouldn't be here to—'

'Little pitchers have big ears,' Ma said. She meant that he must not frighten Mary and Laura.

'Well, all's well that ends well,' Pa replied. 'And those wolves are miles from here by now.'

'What made them act like that?' Laura asked him.

'I don't know, Laura,' he said. 'I guess they had just eaten all they could hold, and they were on their way to the creek to get a drink. Or perhaps they were out playing on the prairie, and not paying any attention to anything but their play, like little girls do sometimes. Perhaps they saw that I didn't have my gun and couldn't do them any harm. Or perhaps they had never seen a man before and didn't know that men can do them any harm. So they didn't think about me at all.'

Pet and Patty were restlessly walking round and round, inside the barn. Jack walked around the camp fire. When he stood still to smell the air and listen, the hair lifted on his neck.

'Bedtime for little girls!' Ma said, cheerfully. Not even Baby Carrie was sleepy yet, but Ma took them all into the house. She told Mary and Laura to go to bed, and she put Baby Carrie's little nightgown on and laid her in the big bed. Then she went outdoors to do the dishes. Laura wanted Pa and Main the house. They seemed so far away outside.

Mary and Laura were good and lay still, but Carrie sat up and played by herself in the dark. In the dark Pa's arm came from behind the quilt in the doorway and quietly took away his gun. Out by the camp fire the tin plates rattled. Then a knife scraped the spider. Ma and Pa were talking together and Laura smelled tobacco smoke.

The house was safe, but it did not feel safe because Pa's gun was not over the door and there was no door; there was only the quilt.

After a long time Ma lifted the quilt. Baby Carrie was asleep then. Ma and Pa came in very quietly and very quietly went to bed. Jack lay across the doorway, but his chin was not on his paws. His head was up, listening. Ma breathed softly, Pa breathed heavily, and Mary was asleep, too. But Laura strained her eyes in the dark to watch Jack. She could not tell whether the hair was standing up on his neck.

Suddenly she was sitting straight up in bed. She had been asleep. The dark was gone. Moonlight streamed through the window hole and streaks of moonlight came through every crack in that wall. Pa stood black in the moonlight at the window. He had his gun.

Right in Laura's ear a wolf howled.

She scringed away from the wall. The wolf was on the other side of it. Laura was too scared to make a sound. The cold was not in her backbone only, it was all through her. Mary pulled the quilt over her head. Jack growled and showed his teeth at the quilt in the doorway.

'Be still, Jack,' Pa said.

Terrible howls curled all around inside the house, and Laura rose out of bed. She wanted to go to Pa, but she knew better than to bother him now. He turned his head and saw her standing in her nightgown.

'Want to see them, Laura?' he asked softly. Laura couldn't say anything, but she nodded, and padded across the ground to him. He stood his gun against the wall and lifted her up to the window hole.

There in the moonlight sat half a circle of wolves. They sat on their haunches and looked at Laura in the window, and she looked at them. She had never seen such big wolves. The biggest one was taller than Laura. He was taller even than Mary. He sat in the middle, exactly opposite Laura. Everything about him was big—his pointed ears, and his pointed mouth with the tongue hanging out, and his strong shoulders and legs, and his two paws side by side, and his tail curled around the squatting haunch. His coat was shaggy grey and his eyes were glittering green.

Laura clutched her toes into a crack of the wall and she folded her arms on the window slab, and she looked and looked at that wolf. But she did not put her head through the empty window space into the outdoors where all those wolves sat so near her, shifting their paws and licking their chops. Pa stood firm against her back and kept his arm tight around her middle.

'He's awful big,' Laura whispered.

'Yes, and see how his coat shines,' Pa whispered into her hair. The moonlight made little glitters in the edges of the shaggy fur, all around the big wolf.

'They are in a ring clear around the house,' Pa whispered. Laura pattered beside him to the other window. He leaned his gun against that wall and lifted her up again. There, sure enough, was the other half of the circle of wolves. All their eyes glittered green in the shadow of the house. Laura could hear their breathing. When they saw Pa and Laura looking out, the middle of the circle moved back a little way.

Pet and Patty were squealing and running inside the barn. Their hoofs pounded the ground and crashed against the walls.

After a moment Pa went back to the other window, and Laura went, too. They were just in time to see the big wolf lift his nose till it pointed straight at the sky. His mouth opened, and a long howl rose towards the moon.

Then all around the house the circle of wolves pointed their noses towards the sky and answered him. Their howls shuddered through the house and filled the moonlight and quavered away across the vast silence of the prairie.

'Now go back to bed, little half-pint,' Pa said. 'Go to sleep. Jack and I will take care of you all.'

So Laura went back to bed. But for a long time she did not sleep. She lay and listened to the breathing of the wolves on the other side of the log wall. She heard the scratch of their claws on the ground, and the snufing of a nose at a crack. She heard the big grey leader howl again, and all the others answering him.

But Pa was walking quietly from one window hole to the other, and Jack did not stop pacing up and down before the quilt that hung in the doorway. The wolves might howl, but they could not get in while Pa and Jack were there. So at last Laura fell asleep.

8

Two Stout Doors

Laura felt a soft warmth on her face and opened her eyes into morning sunshine. Mary was talking to Ma by the camp fire. Laura ran outdoors, all bare inside her nightgown. There were no wolves to be seen; only their tracks were thick around the house and the stable.

Pa came whistling up the creek road. He put his gun on its pegs and led Pet and Patty to the creek to drink as usual. He had followed the wolf tracks so far that he knew they were far away now, following a herd of deer.

The mustangs shied at the wolves' tracks and pricked their ears nervously, and Pet kept her colt close at her side. But they went willingly with Pa, who knew there was nothing to fear.

Breakfast was ready. When Pa came back from the creek they all sat by the fire and ate fried mush and prairie-chicken hash. Pa said he would make a door that very day. He wanted more than a quilt between them and the wolves, next time.

'I have no more nails, but I'll not keep on waiting till I can make a trip to Independence,' he said. 'A man doesn't need nails to build a house or make a door.'

After breakfast he hitched up Pet and Patty, and taking his axe he went to get timber for the door. Laura helped wash the dishes and make the beds, but that day Mary minded the baby. Laura helped Pa make the door. Mary watched, but Laura handed him his tools.

With the saw he sawed logs the right length for a door. He sawed shorter lengths for cross-pieces. Then with the axe he split the logs into slabs, and smoothed them nicely. He laid the long slabs together on the ground and placed the shorter slabs across them. Then with the auger he bored holes through the cross-pieces into the long slabs. Into every hole he drove a wooden peg that fitted tightly.

That made the door. It was a good oak door, solid and strong.

For the hinges he cut three long straps. One hinge was to be near the top of the door, one near the bottom, and one in the middle.

He fastened them first on the door, in this way: he laid a little piece of wood on the door, and bored a hole through it into the door. Then he doubled one end of a strap around the little piece of wood, and with his knife cut round holes through the strap. He laid the little piece of wood on the door again, with the strap doubled around it, and all the holes making one hole. Then Laura gave him a peg and the hammer, and he drove the peg into the hole. The peg went through the strap and the little piece of wood and through the strap again and into the door. That held the strap so that it couldn't get loose.

'I told you a fellow doesn't need nails!' Pa said.

When he had fastened the three hinges to the door, he set the door in the doorway. It fitted. Then he pegged strips of wood to the old slabs on either side of the doorway, to keep the door from swinging outward. He set the door in place again, and Laura stood against it to hold it there, while Pa fastened the hinges to the doorframe.

But before he did this he had made the latch on the door, because, of course, there must be some way to keep a door shut.

This was the way he made the latch: first he hewed a short, thick piece of oak. From one side of this, in the middle, he cut a wide, deep notch. He pegged this stick to the inside of the door, up and down and near the edge. He put the notched side against the door, so that the notch made a little slot.

Then he hewed and whittled a longer, smaller stick. This stick was small enough to slip easily through the slot. He slid one end of it through the slot, and he pegged the other end to the door.

But he did not peg it tightly. The peg was solid and firm in the door, but the hole in the stick was larger than the peg. The only thing that held the stick on the door was the slot.

This stick was the latch. It turned easily on the peg, and its loose end moved up and down in the slot. And the loose end of it was long enough to go through the slot and across the crack between the door and the wall, and to lie against the wall when the door was shut.

When Pa and Laura had hung the door in the doorway, Pa marked the spot on the wall where the end of the latch came. Over that spot he pegged to the wall a stout piece of oak. This piece of oak was cut out at the top, so that the latch could drop between it and the wall.

Now Laura pushed the door shut, and while she pushed she lifted the end of the latch as high as it would go in the slot. Then she let it fall into its place behind the stout piece of oak. That held the latch against the wall, and the up-and-down strip held the latch in its slot against the door.

Nobody could break in without breaking the strong latch in two.

But there must be a way to lift the latch from the outside. So Pa made the latch-string. He cut it from a long strip of good leather. He tied one end to the latch, between the peg and the slot. Above the latch he bored a small hole through the door, and he pushed the end of the latchstring through the hole.

Laura stood outside, and when the end of the latchstring came through the hole she took hold of it and pulled. She could pull it hard enough to lift the latch and let herself in.

The door was finished. It was strong and solid, made of thick oak with oak slabs across it, all pegged together with good stout pegs. The latch-string was out; if you wanted to come in, you pulled the latch-string. But if you were inside and wanted to keep anyone out, then you pulled the latch-string in through its hole and nobody could get in. There was no doorknob on that door, and there was no keyhole and no key. But it was a good door.

'I call that a good day's work!' said Pa. 'And I had a fine little helper!'

He hugged the top of Laura's head with his hand. Then he gathered up his tools and put them away, whistling, and he went to take Pet and Patty from their picket-lines to water. The sun was setting, the breeze was cooler, and supper cooking on the fire made the best supper-smells that Laura had ever smelled.

There was salt pork for supper. It was the last of the salt pork, so next day Pa went hunting. But the day after that he and Laura made the barn door.

It was exactly like the house door, except that it had no latch. Pet and Patty did not understand door-latches and would not pull a latch-string in at night. So instead of a latch Pa made a hole through the door, and he put a chain through the hole.

At night he would pull an end of the chain through a crack between the logs in the stable wall, and he would padlock the two ends of the chain together. Then nobody could get into that stable.

'Now we're all snug!' Pa said. When neighbours began to come into a country, it was best to lock up your horses at night, because, where there are deer there will be wolves, and where there are horses, there will be horse-thieves.

That night at supper Pa said to Ma, 'Now, Caroline, as soon as we get Edwards' house up, I'm going to build you a fireplace, so you can do your cooking in the house, out of the wind and the storms. It seems like I never did see a place with so much sunshine, but I suppose it's bound to rain sometime.'

'Yes, Charles,' Ma said. 'Good weather never lasts for ever on this earth.'

9

A Fire on the Hearth

Outside the house, close to the log wall opposite the door, Pa cut away the grass and scraped the ground smooth. He was getting ready to build the fireplace.

Then he and Ma put the wagon-box on the wheels again, and Pa hitched up Pet and Patty.

The rising sun was shortening all the shadows. Hundreds of meadow larks were rising from the prairie, singing higher and higher in the air. Their songs came down from the great clear sky like a rain of music. And all over the land, where the grasses waved and murmured under the wind, thousands of little dickie-birds clung with their tiny claws to the blossoming weeds and sang their thousands of little songs.

Pet and Patty sniffed the wind and whinnied with joy. They arched their necks and pawed at the ground because they were eager to go. Pa was whistling while he climbed to the wagon-seat and took up the reins. Then he looked down at Laura, who was looking up at him, and he stopped whistling and said: 'Want to go along, Laura? You and Mary?'

Ma said they could. They climbed up the wheels, clinging to the spokes with their bare toes, and they sat on the high wagon-seat beside Pa. Pet and Patty started with a little jump, and the wagon went jolting down the road that Pa's wagon wheels had made.

They went down between the bare, reddish-yellow walls of earth, all ridged and wrinkled by forgotten rains. Then they went on, across the rolling land of the creek bottoms. Masses of trees covered some of the low, rounded hills, and some of them were grassy, open spaces. Deer were lying in the shadows of the trees, and deer were grazing in the sunshine on the green grass. They lifted their heads and pricked their ears, and stood chewing and watching the wagon with their soft, large eyes.

All along the road the wild larkspur was blossoming pink and blue and white, birds balanced on yellow plumes of goldenrod, and butterflies were fluttering. Starry daisies lighted the shadows under trees, squirrels chattered on branches overhead, white-tailed rabbits hopped along the road, and snakes wriggled quickly across it when they heard the wagon coming.

Deep in the lowest valley the creek was running, in the shadow of dirt bluffs. When Laura looked up those bluffs, she couldn't see the prairie grass at all. Trees grew up the bluffs where the earth had crumbled, and where the bare dirt was so steep that trees couldn't grow on it bushes held on desperately with their roots. Half-naked roots were high above Laura's head.

'Where are the Indian camps?' Laura asked Pa. He had seen the Indians' deserted camps, here among the bluffs. But he was too busy to show them to her now. He must get the rocks to build the fireplace.

'You girls can play,' he said, 'but don't go out of my sight and don't go into the water. And don't play with snakes. Some of the snakes down here are poison.'

So Laura and Mary played by the creek, while Pa dug the rocks he wanted and loaded them into the wagon.

They watched long-legged water-bugs skate over the

glassy-still pools. They ran along the bank to scare the frogs, and laughed when the green-coated frogs with their white vests plopped into the water. They listened to the wood-pigeons call among the trees, and the brown thrush singing. They saw the little minnows swimming all together in the shallow places where the creek ran sparkling. The minnows were thin grey shadows in the rippling water, only now and again one minnow flashed the sunshine from its silvery belly.

There was no wind along the creek. The air was still and drowsy-warm. It smelled of damp roots and mud, and it was full of the sound of rustling leaves and of the water running.

In the muddy places where deer's tracks were thick and every hoofprint held water, swarms of mosquitoes rose up with a keen, sharp buzzing. Laura and Mary slapped at mosquitoes on their faces and necks and hands and legs, and wished they could go wading. They were so hot and the water looked so cool. Laura was sure that it would do no harm just to dip one foot in, and when Pa's back was turned she almost did it.

'Laura,' said Pa, and she snatched the naughty foot back.

'If you girls want to go wading,' Pa said, 'you can do it in that shallow place. Don't go in over your ankles.'

Mary waded only a little while. She said the gravel hurt her feet, and she sat on a log and patiently slapped at mosquitoes. But Laura slapped and kept on wading. When she stepped, the gravel hurt her feet. When she stood still, the tiny minnows swarmed about her toes and nibbled them with their tiny mouths. It was a funny, squiggling feeling. Laura tried and tried to catch a minnow, but she only got the hem of her dress wet.

Then the wagon was loaded. Pa called, 'Come along, girls!' and they climbed to the wagon-seat again and rode away from the creek. Up through the woods and hills they rode again, to the High Prairie where the winds were always blowing and the grasses seemed to sing and whisper and laugh.

They had had a wonderful time in the creek bottoms. But Laura liked the High Prairie best. The prairie was so wide and sweet and clean.

That afternoon Ma sat sewing in the shade of the house, and Baby Carrie played on the quilt beside her, while Laura and Mary watched Pa build the fireplace.

First he mixed clay and water to a beautiful thick mud, in the mustangs' water bucket. He let Laura stir the mud while he laid a row of rocks around three sides of the space he had cleared by the house-wall. Then with a wooden paddle he spread the mud over the rocks. In the mud he laid another row of rocks, and plastered them over the top and down on the inside with more mud.

He made a box on the ground; three sides of the box were made of rocks and mud, and the other side was the log wall of the house.

With rocks and mud and more rocks and more mud, he built the walls as high as Laura's chin. Then on the walls, close against the house, he laid a log. He plastered the log all over with mud.

After that, he built up rocks and mud on top of that log. He was making the chimney now, and he made it smaller and smaller.

He had to go to the creek for more rocks. Laura and Mary could not go again, because Ma said the damp air might give them a fever. Mary sat beside Ma and sewed another block of her nine-patch quilt, but Laura mixed another bucketful of mud.

Next day Pa built the chimney as high as the housewall. Then he stood and looked at it. He ran his fingers through his hair.

'You look like a wild man, Charles,' Ma said. 'You're standing your hair all on end.'

'It stands on end, anyway, Caroline,' Pa answered. 'When I was courting you, it never would lie down, no matter how much I slicked it with bear grease.'

He threw himself down on the grass at her feet. 'I'm plumb tuckered out, lifting rocks up there.'

'You've done well to build that chimney up so high, all by yourself,' Ma said. She ran her hand through his hair and stood it up more than ever. 'Why don't you make it stick-and-daub the rest of the way?' she asked him.

'Well, it would be easier,' he admitted. 'I'm blamed if I don't believe I will!'

He jumped up. Ma said, 'Oh, stay here in the shade and rest awhile.' But he shook his head.

'No use lazing here while there's work to be done, Caroline. The sooner I get the fireplace done, the sooner you can do your cooking inside, out of the wind.'

He hauled saplings from the woods, and he cut and notched them and laid them up like the walls of the house, on top of the stone chimney. As he laid them, he plastered them well with mud. And that finished the chimney.

Then he went into the house, and with his axe and saw he cut a hole in the wall. He cut away the logs that had made the fourth wall at the bottom of the chimney. And there was the fireplace.

It was large enough for Laura and Mary and Baby Carrie to sit in. Its bottom was the ground that Pa had cleared of grass, and its front was the space where Pa had cut away the logs. Across the top of that space was the log that Pa had plastered all over with mud.

On each side Pa pegged a thick slab of green oak against the cut ends of the logs. Then by the upper corners of the fireplace he pegged chunks of oak to the wall, and on these he laid an oak slab and pegged it firmly. That was the mantel-shelf.

As soon as it was done, Ma set in the middle of the mantel-shelf the little china woman she had brought from the Big Woods. The little china woman had come all the way and had not been broken. She stood on the mantelshelf with her little china shoes and her wide china skirts and her tight china bodice, and her pink cheeks and blue eyes and golden hair all made of china.

Then Pa and Ma and Mary and Laura stood and admired that fireplace. Only Carrie did not care about it. She pointed at the little china woman and yelled when Mary and Laura told her that no one but Ma could touch it.

'You'll have to be careful with your fire, Caroline,' Pa said. 'We don't want sparks going up the chimney to set the roof on fire. That cloth would burn, easy. I'll split out some clapboards as soon as I can, and make a roof you won't have to worry about.'

So Ma carefully built a little fire in the new fireplace, and she roasted a prairie hen for supper. And that evening they ate in the house.

They sat at table, by the western window. Pa had quickly made the table of two slabs of oak. One end of the slabs stuck in a crack of the wall, and the other ends rested on short, upright logs. Pa had smoothed the slabs with his axe, and the table was very nice when Ma spread a cloth over it.

The chairs were chunks of big logs. The floor was the earth that Ma had swept clean with her willow-bough broom. On the floor, in the corners, the beds were neat under their patchwork quilts. The rays of the setting sun came through the window and filled the house with golden light.

Outside, and far, far away to the pink edge of the sky, the wind went blowing and the wild grasses waved.

Inside, the house was pleasant. The good roast chicken was juicy in Laura's mouth. Her hands and face were washed, her hair was combed, her napkin was tied around her neck.

She sat up straight on the round end of log and used her knife and fork nicely, as Ma had taught her. She did not say anything, because children must not speak at table until they are spoken to, but she looked at Pa and Ma and Mary and at Baby Carrie in Ma's lap, and she felt contented. It was nice to be living in a house again.

10

A Roof and a Floor

All day long, every day, Laura and Mary were busy. When the dishes were washed and the beds made, there was always plenty to do and to see and to listen to.

They hunted for birds' nests in the tall grass, and when they found them the mother birds squawked and scolded. Sometimes they touched a nest gently, and all in an instant a nest full of downiness became a nest full of wide-gaping beaks, hungrily squawking. Then the mother bird scolded like anything, and Mary and Laura quietly went away because they did not want to worry her too much.

In the tall grass they lay still as mice and watched flocks of little prairie chickens running and pecking around their anxiously clucking, smooth brown mothers. They watched striped snakes rippling between the grass stems or lying so still that only their tiny flickering tongues and glittering eyes showed that they were alive. They were garter snakes and would not hurt anybody, but Laura and Mary did not touch them. Ma said snakes were best left alone, because some snakes would bite, and it was better to be safe than sorry.

And sometimes there'd be a great grey rabbit, so still in the lights and shadows of a grass clump that you were near enough to touch him before you saw him. Then, if you were very quiet, you might stand a long time looking at him. His round eyes stared at yours without meaning anything. His nose wiggled, and sunlight was rosy through his long ears, that had delicate veins in them and the softest short fur on their outsides. The rest of his fur was so thick and soft that at last you couldn't help trying, very carefully, to touch it.

Then he was gone in a flash and the place where he had been sitting was hollowed and smooth and still warm from his warm behind.

All the time, of course, Laura or Mary was minding Baby Carrie, except when she had her afternoon nap. Then they sat and soaked in the sunshine and the wind until Laura forgot that the baby was sleeping. She jumped up and ran and shouted till Ma came to the door and said, 'Dear me, Laura, must you yell like an Indian? I declare,' Ma said, 'if you girls aren't getting to look like Indians! Can I never teach you to keep your sun-bonnets on?'

Pa was up on the house wall, beginning the roof. He looked down at them and laughed.

'One little Indian, two little Indians, three little Indians,' he sang softly. 'No, only two.'

'You make three,' Mary said to him. 'You're brown, too.'

'But you aren't little, Pa,' said Laura. 'Pa, when are we going to see a papoose?'

'Goodness!' Ma exclaimed. 'What do you want to see an Indian baby for? Put on your sun-bonnet, now, and forget such nonsense.'

Laura's sun-bonnet hung down her back. She pulled it up by its strings, and its sides came past her cheeks. When her sun-bonnet was on she could see only what was in front of her, and that was why she was always pushing it back and letting it hang by its strings tied around her throat. She put her sun-bonnet on when Ma told her to, but she did not forget the papoose.

This was Indian country and she didn't know why she didn't see Indians. She knew she would see them sometime, though. Pa said so, but she was getting tired of waiting.

Pa had taken the canvas wagon-top off the house, and now he was ready to put the roof on. For days and days he had been hauling logs from the creek bottoms and splitting them into thin, long slabs. Piles of slabs lay all around the house and slabs stood against it.

'Come out of the house, Caroline,' he said. 'I don't want to risk anything falling on you or Carrie.'

'Wait, Charles, till I put away the china Shepherdess,' Ma answered. In a minute she came out, with a quilt and her mending and Baby Carrie. She spread the quilt on the shady grass by the stable, and sat there to do her mending and watch Carrie play.

Pa reached down and pulled up a slab. He laid it across the ends of the sapling rafters. Its edge stuck out beyond the wall. Then Pa put some nails in his mouth and took his hammer out of his belt, and he began to nail the slab to the rafters.

Mr Edwards had lent him the nails. They had met in the woods, where they were both chopping down trees, and Mr Edwards had insisted that Pa borrow nails for the roof.

'That's what I call a good neighbour!' Pa said when he told Ma about it.

'Yes,' said Ma. 'But I don't like to be beholden, not even to the best of neighbours.'

'Nor I,' Pa replied. 'I've never been beholden to any man yet, and I never will be. But neighbourliness is another matter, and I'll pay him back every nail as soon as I can make the trip to Independence.'

Now Pa carefully took the nails one by one from his mouth, and with ringing blows of the hammer he drove them into the slab. It was much quicker than drilling holes and whittling pegs and driving them into the holes. But every now and then a nail sprang away from the tough oak when the hammer hit it, and if Pa was not holding it firmly, it went sailing through the air.

Then Mary and Laura watched it fall, and they searched in the grass till they found it. Sometimes it was bent. Then Pa carefully pounded it straight again. It would never do to lose or waste a nail.

When Pa had nailed down two slabs, he got up on them. He laid and nailed more slabs, all the way up to the top of the rafters. The edge of each slab lapped over the edge of the slab below it.

Then he began again on the other side of the house, and he laid the roof all the way up from that side. A little crack was left between the highest slabs. So Pa made a little trough of two slabs, and he nailed this trough firmly, upside down over the crack.

The roof was done. The house was darker than it had been, because no light came through the slabs. There was not one single crack that would let rain come in.

'You have done a splendid job, Charles,' Ma said, 'and I'm thankful to have a good roof over my head.'

'You shall have furniture, too, as fine as I can make it,' Pa replied. 'I'll make a bedstead as soon as the floor is laid.'

He began again to haul logs. Day after day he hauled logs. He did not even stop hauling logs to go hunting; he took his gun on the wagon and brought back at night whatever meat he had shot from the wagon-seat.

When he had hauled enough logs to make the floor, he began to split them. He split each log straight down the middle. Laura liked to sit on the woodpile and watch him.

First, with a mighty blow of his axe he split the butt of the log. Into the crack he slipped the thin edge of an iron wedge. Then he wrenched the axe out of the log, and he drove the wedge deeper into the crack. The tough wood split a little farther.

All the way up the log Pa fought that tough oak. He struck

with his axe into the crack. He drove blocks of wood into it, and moved the iron wedge higher. Little by little he followed the crack up the log.

He swung the axe high, and brought it down with a great swing and a grunt from his chest. 'Ugh!' The axe whizzed and struck, plung! It always struck exactly where Pa wanted it to.

At last, with a tearing, cracking sound, the whole log split. Its two halves lay on the ground, showing the tree's pale insides and the darker streak up its middle. Then Pa wiped the sweat from his forehead, he took a fresh grip on the axe, and he tackled another log.

One day the last log was split, and next morning Pa began to lay the floor. He dragged the logs into the house and laid them one by one, flat side up. With his spade he scraped the ground underneath, and fitted the round side of the log firmly down into it. With his axe he trimmed away the edge of bark and cut the wood straight, so that each log fitted against the next, with hardly a crack between them.

Then he took the head of the axe in his hand, and with little, careful blows he smoothed the wood. He squinted along the log to see that the surface was straight and true. He took off last little bits, here and there. Finally he ran his hand over the smoothness, and nodded.

'Not a Splinter!' he said. 'That'll be all right for little bare feet to run over.'

He left that log fitted into its place, and dragged in another.

When he came to the fireplace, he used shorter logs. He left a space of bare earth for a hearth, so that when sparks or coals popped out of the fire they would not burn the floor.

One day the floor was done. It was smooth and firm and hard, a good floor of solid oak that would last, Pa said, for ever.

'You can't beat a good puncheon floor,' he said, and Ma

said she was glad to be up off the dirt. She put the little china woman on the mantel-shelf, and spread a red checked cloth on the table.

'There,' she said. 'Now we're living like civilized folks again.'

After that Pa filled the cracks in the walls. He drove thin strips of wood into them, and plastered them well with mud, filling every chink.

'That's a good job,' Ma said. 'That chinking will keep out the wind, no matter how hard it blows.'

Pa stopped whistling to smile at her. He slapped the last bit of mud between the logs and smoothed it and set down the bucket. At last the house was finished.

'I wish we had glass for the windows,' Pa said.

'We don't need glass, Charles,' said Ma.

'Just the same, if I do well with my hunting and trapping this winter, I'm going to get some glass in Independence next spring,' said Pa. 'And hang the expense!'

'Glass windows would be nice if we can afford them,' Ma said. 'But we'll cross that bridge when we come to it.'

They were all happy that night. The fire on the hearth was pleasant, for on the High Prairie even the summer nights were cool. The red-checked cloth was on the table, the little china woman glimmered on the mantel-shelf, and the new floor was golden in the flickering firelight. Outside, the night was large and full of stars. Pa sat for a long time in the door-way and played his fiddle and sang to Ma and Mary and Laura in the house and to the starry night outside.

11

Indians in the House

Early one morning Pa took his gun and went hunting. He had meant to make the bedstead that day. He had brought in the slabs, when Ma said she had no meat for dinner. So he stood the slabs against the wall and took down his gun.

Jack wanted to go hunting, too. His eyes begged Pa to take him, and whines came up from his chest and quivered in his throat till Laura almost cried with him. But Pa chained him to the stable.

'No, Jack,' Pa said. 'You must stay here and guard the place.' Then he said to Mary and Laura, 'Don't let him loose, girls.'

Poor Jack lay down. It was a disgrace to be chained, and he felt it deeply. He turned his head from Pa and would not watch him going away with the gun on his shoulder. Pa went farther and farther away, till the prairies swallowed him and he was gone.

Laura tried to comfort Jack, but he would not be comforted. The more he thought about the chain, the worse he felt. Laura tried to cheer him up to frisk and play, but he only grew more sullen.

Both Mary and Laura felt that they could not leave Jack while he was so unhappy. So all that morning they stayed by the stable. They stroked Jack's smooth, brindled head and scratched around his ears, and told him how sorry they were that he must be chained. He licked their hands a little bit, but he was very sad and angry.

His head was on Laura's knee and she was talking to him, when suddenly he stood up and growled a fierce, deep growl. The hair on his neck stood straight up and his eyes glared red.

Laura was frightened. Jack had never growled at her before. Then she looked over her shoulder, where Jack was looking, and she saw two naked, wild men coming, one behind the other, on the Indian trail.

'Mary! Look!' she cried. Mary looked and saw them, too.

They were tall, thin, fierce-looking men. Their skin was brownish-red. Their heads seemed to go up to a peak, and the peak was a tuft of hair that stood straight up and ended in feathers. Their eyes were black and still and glittering, like snakes' eyes.

They came closer and closer. Then they went out of sight, on the other side of the house.

Laura's head turned and so did Mary's, and they looked at the place where those terrible men would appear when they came past the house.

'Indians!' Mary whispered. Laura was shivery; there was a queer feeling in her middle and the bones in her legs felt weak. She wanted to sit down. But she stood and looked and waited for those Indians to come out from beyond the house. The Indians did not do that.

All this time Jack had been growling. Now he stopped growling and was lunging against the chain. His eyes were red and his lips curled back and all the hair on his back was bristling. He bounded and bounded, clear off the ground, trying to get loose from the chain. Laura was glad that the chain kept him right there with her.

'Jack's here,' she whispered to Mary. 'Jack won't let them hurt us. We'll be safe if we stay close to Jack.'

'They are in the house,' Mary whispered. 'They are in the house with Ma and Carrie.'

Then Laura began to shake all over. She knew she must do something. She did not know what those Indians were doing to Ma and Baby Carrie. There was no sound at all from the house.

'Oh, what are they doing to Ma!' she screamed, in a whisper.

'Oh, I don't know!' Mary whispered.

'I'm going to let Jack loose,' Laura whispered hoarsely. 'Jack will kill them.'

'Pa said not to,' Mary answered. They were too scared to speak out loud. They put their heads together and watched the house and whispered.

'He didn't know Indians would come,' Laura said.

'He said not to let Jack loose.' Mary was almost crying.

Laura thought of little Baby Carrie and Ma, shut in the house with those Indians. She said, 'I'm going in to help Ma!'

She ran two steps, and walked a step, then she turned and flew back to Jack. She clutched him wildly and hung on to his strong, panting neck. Jack wouldn't let anything hurt her.

'We mustn't leave Ma in there alone,' Mary whispered. She stood still and trembled. Mary never could move when she was frightened. Laura hid her face against Jack and held on to him tightly.

Then she made her arms let go. Her hands balled into fists and her eyes shut tight and she ran towards the house as fast as she could run.

She stumbled and fell down and her eyes popped open. She was up again and running before she could think. Mary was close behind her. They came to the door. It was open, and they slipped into the house without a sound.

The naked wild men stood by the fireplace. Ma was bending over the fire, cooking something. Carrie clung to Ma's skirts with both hands and her head was hidden in the folds.

Laura ran towards Ma, but just as she reached the hearth she smelled a horribly bad smell and she looked up at the Indians. Quick as a flash, she ducked behind the long, narrow slab that leaned against the wall.

The slab was just wide enough to cover both her eyes. If she held her head perfectly still and pressed her nose against the slab, she couldn't see the Indians. And she felt safer. But she couldn't help moving her head just a little, so that one eye peeped out and she could see the wild men.

First she saw their leather moccasins. Then their stringy, bare, red-brown legs, all the way up. Around their waists each of the Indians wore a leather thong, and the furry skin of a small animal hung down in front. The fur was striped black and white, and now Laura knew what made that smell. The skins were fresh skunk skins.

A knife like Pa's hunting-knife, and a hatchet like Pa's hatchet, were stuck into each skunk skin.

The Indian's ribs made little ridges up their bare sides. Their arms were folded on their chests. At last Laura looked again at their faces, and she dodged quickly behind the slab.

Their faces were bold and fierce and terrible. Their black eyes glittered. High on their foreheads and above their ears where hair grows, these wild men had no hair. But on top of their heads a tuft of hair stood straight up. It was wound around with string, and feathers were stuck in it.

When Laura peeked out from behind the slab again, both Indians were looking straight at her. Her heart jumped into her throat and choked her with its pounding. Two black eyes glittered down into her eyes. The Indian did not move, not one muscle of his face moved. Only his eyes shone and sparkled at her. Laura didn't move, either. She didn't even breathe.

The Indian made two short, harsh sounds in his throat. The other Indian made one sound, like 'Hah!' Laura hid her eyes behind the slab again.

She heard Ma take the cover off the bake-oven. She heard the Indians squat down on the hearth. After a while she heard them eating.

Laura peeked, and hid, and peeked again, while the Indians ate the cornbread that Ma had baked. They ate every morsel of it, and even picked up the crumbs from the hearth. Ma stood and watched them and stroked Baby Carrie's head. Mary stood close behind Ma and held on to her sleeve.

Faintly Laura heard Jack's chain rattling. Jack was still trying to get loose.

When every crumb of the cornbread was gone, the Indians rose up. The skunk smell was stronger when they moved. One of them made harsh sounds in his throat again. Ma looked at him with big eyes; she did not say anything. The Indian turned around, the other Indian turned, too, and they walked across the floor and out through the door. Their feet made no sound at all.

Ma sighed a long, long sigh. She hugged Laura tight in one arm and Mary tight in the other arm, and through the window they watched those Indians going away, one behind the other, on the dim trail towards the west. Then Ma sat down on the bed and hugged Laura and Mary tighter, and trembled. She looked sick.

'Do you feel sick, Ma?' Mary asked her.

'No,' said Ma. 'I'm just thankful they're gone.'

Laura wrinkled her nose and said, 'They smell awful.'

'That was the skunk skins they wore,' Ma said.

Then they told her how they had left Jack and had come into the house because they were afraid the Indians would hurt her and Baby Carrie. Ma said they were her brave little girls.

'Now we must get dinner,' she said. 'Pa will be here soon and we must have dinner ready for him. Mary, bring me some wood. Laura, you may set the table.'

Ma rolled up her sleeves and washed her hands and mixed

cornbread, while Mary brought the wood and Laura set the table. She set a tin plate and knife and fork and cup for Pa, and the same for Ma, with Carrie's little tin cup beside Ma's. And she set tin plates and knives and forks for her and Mary, but only their one cup between the plates.

Ma made the cornmeal and water into two thin loaves, each shaped in a half circle. She laid the loaves with their straight sides together in the bake-oven, and she pressed her hand flat on top of each loaf. Pa always said he did not ask any other sweetening, when Ma put the prints of her hands on the loaves.

Laura had hardly set the table when Pa was there. He left a big rabbit and two prairie hens outside the door, and stepped in and laid his gun on its pegs. Laura and Mary ran and clutched him, both talking at once.

'What's all this? What's all this?' he said, rumpling their hair. 'Indians? So you've seen Indians at last, have you, Laura? I noticed they have a camp in a little valley west of here. Did Indians come to the house, Caroline?'

'Yes, Charles, two of them,' Ma said. 'I'm sorry, but they took all your tobacco, and they ate a lot of cornbread. They pointed to the cornmeal and made signs for me to cook some. I was afraid not to. Oh Charles! I was afraid!'

'You did the right thing,' Pa told her. 'We don't want to make enemies of any Indians.' Then he said, 'Whew! what a smell.'

'They wore fresh skunk skins,' said Ma. 'And that was all they wore.'

'Must have been thick while they were here,' Pa said.

'It was, Charles. We were short of cornmeal, too.'

'Oh well. We have enough to hold out a while yet. And our meat is running all over the country. Don't worry, Caroline.'

'But they took all your tobacco.'

'Never mind,' Pa said. 'I'll get along without tobacco till

I can make that trip to Independence. The main thing is to be on good terms with the Indians. We don't want to wake up some night with a band of screeching dev—'

He stopped. Laura dreadfully wanted to know what he had been going to say. But Ma's lips were pressed together and she shook a little shake of her head at Pa.

'Come on, Mary and Laura!' Pa said. 'We'll skin that rabbit and dress the prairie hens while that cornbread bakes. Hurry! I'm hungry as a wolf!'

They sat on the woodpile in the wind and sunshine and watched Pa work with his hunting-knife. The big rabbit was shot through the eye, and the prairie hens' heads were shot clean away. They never knew what hit them, Pa said.

Laura held the edge of the rabbit skin while Pa's keen knife ripped it off the rabbit meat. I'll salt this skin and peg it out on the house wall to dry,' he said. 'It will make a warm fur cap for some little girl to wear next winter.'

But Laura could not forget the Indians. She said to Pa that if they had turned Jack loose, he would have eaten those Indians right up.

Pa laid down the knife. 'Did you girls even think of turning Jack loose?' he asked, in a dreadful voice.

Laura's head bowed down and she whispered, 'Yes, Pa.'

'After I told you not to?' Pa said, in a more dreadful voice.

Laura couldn't speak, but Mary choked, 'Yes, Pa.'

For a moment Pa was silent. He sighed a long sigh like Ma's sigh after the Indians went away.

'After this,' he said, in a terrible voice, 'you girls remember always to do as you're told. Don't you even think of disobeying me. Do you hear?'

'Yes, Pa,' Laura and Mary whispered.

'Do you know what would have happened if you had tuned Jack loose?' Pa asked.

'No, Pa,' they whispered.

'He would have bitten those Indians,' said Pa. 'Then

there would have been trouble. Bad trouble. Do you under-stand?'

'Yes, Pa,' they said. But they did not understand.

'Would they have killed Jack?' Laura asked.

'Yes. And that's not all. You girls remember this: you do as you're told, no matter what happens.'

'Yes, Pa,' Laura said, and Mary said, 'Yes, Pa.' They were glad they had not turned Jack loose.

'Do as you're told,' said Pa, 'and no harm will come to you.'

12

Fresh Water to Drink

Pa had made the bedstead. He had smoothed the oak slabs till there was not a splinter on them. Then he pegged them firmly together. Four slabs made a box to hold the straw-tick. Across the bottom of it Pa stretched a rope, zigzagged from side to side and pulled tight.

One end of the bedstead Pa pegged solidly to the wall, in a corner of the house. Only one corner of the bed was not against a wall. At this corner, Pa set up a tall slab. He pegged it to the bedstead. As high up as he could reach, he pegged two strips of oak to the walls and to the tall slab. Then he climbed up on them, and pegged the top of the tall slab solidly to a rafter. And on the strips of oak he laid a shelf, above the bed.

'There you are, Caroline!' he said.

'I can't wait to see it made up,' said Ma. 'Help me bring in the straw-tick.'

She had filled the straw-tick that morning. There was no straw on the High Prairie, so she had filled it with dry, clean, dead grass. It was hot from the sunshine and it had a grassy, sweet smell. Pa helped her bring it into the house and lay it in the bedstead. She tucked the sheets in, and spread her prettiest patchwork quilt over them. At the head of the bed she set up the goose-feather pillows, and spread the pillow-shams against them. On each white pillow-sham two little birds were outlined with red thread.

Then Pa and Ma and Laura and Mary stood and looked at the bed. It was a very nice bed. The zigzag rope was softer than the floor to sleep on. The straw-tick was plump with the sweet-smelling grass, the quilt lay smooth, and the pretty pillow-shams stood up crisply. The shelf was a good place to store things. The whole house had quite an air, with such a bed in it.

That night when Ma went to bed, she settled into the crackling straw-tick and said to Pa, 'I declare, I'm so comfortable it's almost sinful.'

Mary and Laura still slept on the floor, but Pa would make a little bed for them as soon as he could. He had made the big bed, and he had made a stout cupboard and padlocked it, so the Indians could not take all the cornmeal if they came again. Now he had only to dig a well, and then he would make that trip to town. He must dig the well first, so that Ma could have water while he was gone.

Next morning he marked a large circle in the grass near the corner of the house. With his spade he cut the sod inside the circle, and lifted it up in large pieces. Then he began to shovel out the earth, digging himself deeper and deeper down.

Mary and Laura must not go near the well while Pa was digging. Even when they couldn't see his head any more, shovelfuls of earth came flying up. At last the spade flew up and fell in the grass. Then Pa jumped. His hands caught hold of the sod, then one elbow gripped it, and then the other elbow, and with a heave Pa came rolling out. 'I can't throw the dirt out from any deeper,' he said.

He had to have help, now. So he took his gun and rode away on Patty. When he came back he brought a plump rabbit, and he had traded work with Mr Scott. Mr Scott would help him dig this well, and then he would help dig Mr Scott's well.

Ma and Laura and Mary had not seen Mr and Mrs Scott.

Their house was hidden somewhere in a little valley on the prairie. Laura had seen the smoke rising up from it, and that was all.

At dawn next morning Mr Scott came. He was short and stout. His hair was bleached by the sun and his skin was bright red and scaly. He did not tan; he peeled.

'It's this blasted sun and wind,' he said. 'Beg your pardon, ma'am, but it's enough to make a saint use strong language. I might as well be a snake, the way I keep on shedding my skin in this country.'

Laura liked him. Every morning, as soon as the dishes were washed and the beds made, she ran out to watch Mr Scott and Pa working at the well. The sunshine was blistering, even the winds were hot, and the prairie grasses were turning yellow. Mary preferred to stay in the house and sew on her patchwork quilt. But Laura liked the fierce light and the sun and the wind, and she couldn't stay away from the well. But she was not allowed to go near its edge.

Pa and Mr Scott had made a stout windlass. It stood over the well, and two buckets hung from it on the ends of a rope. When the windlass was turned, one bucket went down into the well and the other bucket came up. In the morning Mr Scott slid down the rope and dug. He filled the buckets with earth, almost as fast as Pa could haul them up and empty them. After dinner, Pa slid down the rope into the well, and Mr Scott hauled up the buckets.

Every morning, before Pa would let Mr Scott go down the rope, he set a candle in a bucket and lighted it and lowered it to the bottom. Once Laura peeped over the edge and she saw the candle brightly burning, far down in the dark hole in the ground.

Then Pa would say, 'Seems to be all right,' and he would pull up the bucket and blow out the candle.

'That's all foolishness, Ingalls,' Mr Scott said. 'The well was all right yesterday.'

'You can't ever tell,' Pa replied. 'Better be safe than sorry.'

Laura did not know what danger Pa was looking for by that candle-light. She did not ask, because Pa and Mr Scott were busy. She meant to ask later, but she forgot.

One morning Mr Scott came while Pa was eating breakfast. They heard him shout: 'Hi, Ingalls! It's sunup. Let's go!' Pa drank his coffee and went out.

The windlass began to creak and Pa began to whistle. Laura and Mary were washing the dishes and Ma was making the big bed, when Pa's whistling stopped. They heard him say, 'Scott!' He shouted, 'Scott! Scott!' Then he called: 'Caroline! Come quick!'

Ma ran out of the house. Laura ran after her.

'Scott's fainted, or something, down there,' Pa said. 'I've got to go down after him.'

'Did you send down the candle?' Ma asked.

'No. I thought he had. I asked him if it was all right, and he said it was.' Pa cut the empty bucket off the rope and tied the rope firmly to the windlass.

'Charles, you can't. You mustn't,' Ma said.

'Caroline, I've got to.'

'You can't. Oh, Charles, no!'

'I'll make it all right. I won't breathe till I get out. We can't let him die down there.'

Ma said, fiercely: 'Laura, keep back!' So Laura kept back. She stood against the house and shivered.

'No, no, Charles! I can't let you,' Ma said. 'Get on Patty and go for help.'

'There isn't time.'

'Charles, if I can't pull you up—if you keel over down there and I can't pull you up—'

'Caroline, I've got to,' Pa said. He swung into the well. His head slid out of sight, down the rope.

Ma crouched and shaded her eyes, staring down into the well.

All over the prairie meadowlarks were rising, singing, flying straight up into the sky. The wind was blowing warmer, but Laura was cold.

Suddenly Ma jumped up and seized the handle of the windlass. She tugged at it with all her might. The rope strained and the windlass creaked. Laura thought that Pa had keeled over, down in the dark bottom of the well, and Ma couldn't pull him up. But the windlass turned a little, and then a little more.

Pa's hand came up, holding to the rope. His other hand reached above it and took hold of the rope. Then Pa's head came up. His arm held on to the windlass. Then somehow he got to the ground and sat there.

The windlass whirled around and there was a thud deep down in the well. Pa struggled to get up and Ma said: 'Sit still, Charles! Laura, get some water. Quick!'

Laura ran. She came hurrying back, lugging the pail of water. Pa and Ma were both turning the windlass. The rope slowly wound itself up, and the bucket came up out of the well, and tied to the bucket and the rope was Mr Scott. His arms and his legs and his head hung and wobbled, his mouth was partly open and his eyes half shut.

Pa tugged him on to the grass. Pa rolled him over and he flopped where he was rolled. Pa felt his wrist and listened at his chest, and then Pa lay down beside him.

'He's breathing,' Pa said. 'He'll be all right, in the air. I'm all right, Caroline. I'm plumb tuckered out, that's all.'

'Well!' Ma scolded. 'I should think you would be! Of all the senseless performances! My goodness gracious! scaring a body to death, all for want of a little reasonable care! My goodness! I—'She covered her face with her apron and burst out crying.

That was a terrible day.

'I don't want a well,' Ma sobbed. 'It isn't worth it. I won't have you running such risks!'

Mr Scott had breathed a kind of gas that stays deep in the ground. It stays at the bottom of wells because it is heavier than the air. It cannot be seen or smelled, but no one can breathe it very long and live. Pa had gone down into that gas to tie Mr Scott to the rope so that he could be pulled up out of the gas.

When Mr Scott was able, he went home. Before he went he said to Pa: 'You were right about that candle business, Ingalls. I thought it was all foolishness and I would not bother with it, but I've found out my mistake.'

'Well,' said Pa, 'where a light can't live, I know I can't. And I like to be safe when I can be. But all's well that ends well.'

Pa rested awhile. He had breathed a little of the gas and he felt like resting. But that afternoon he unravelled a thread from a tow sack, and he took a little powder from his powder-horn. He tied the powder in a piece of cloth with one end of the tow string in the powder.

'Come along, Laura,' he said, 'and I'll show you something.'

They went to the well. Pa lighted the end of the string and waited till the spark was crawling quickly along it. Then he dropped the little bundle into the well.

In a minute they heard a muffled bang! and a puff of smoke came out of the well. 'That will bring the gas,' Pa said.

When the smoke was all gone, he let Laura light the candle and stand beside him while he let it down. All the way down in the dark hole the little candle kept on burning like a star.

So next day Pa and Mr Scott went on digging the well. But they always sent the candle down every morning.

There began to be a little water in the well, but it was not enough. The buckets came up full of mud, and Pa and Mr Scott worked every day in deeper mud. In the mornings when the candle went down, it lighted oozing-wet walls, and candlelight sparkled in rings over the water when the bucket struck bottom.

Pa stood knee deep in water and bailed out bucketfuls before he could begin digging in the mud.

One day when he was digging, a loud shout came echoing up. Ma ran out of the house and Laura ran to the well. 'Pull, Scott! Pull!' Pa yelled. A swishing, gurgling sound echoed down there. Mr Scott turned the windlass as fast as he could, and Pa, came up climbing hand over hand up the rope.

'I'm blamed if that's not quicksand!' Pa gasped, as he stepped on to the ground, muddy and dripping. 'I was pushing down hard on the spade, when all of a sudden it went down, the whole length of the handle. And water came pouring up all around me.'

'A good six feet of this rope's wet,' Mr Scott said, winding it up. The bucket was full of water. 'You showed sense in getting out of that hand over hand, Ingalls. That water came up faster than I could pull you out.' Then Mr Scott slapped his thigh and shouted, 'I'm blasted if you didn't bring up the spade!'

Sure enough, Pa had saved his spade.

In a little while the well was almost full of water. A circle of blue sky lay not far down in the ground, and when Laura looked at it, a little girl's head looked up at her. When she waved her hand, a hand on the water's surface waved, too.

The water was clear and cold and good. Laura thought she had never tasted anything so good as those long, cold drinks of water. Pa hauled no more stale, warm water from the creek. He built a solid platform over the well, and a heavy cover for the hole that let the water-bucket through. Laura must never touch that cover. But whenever she or Mary was thirsty, Ma lifted the cover and drew a dripping bucket of cold, fresh water from that well.

13

Texas Longhorns

One evening Laura and Pa were sitting on the doorstep. The moon shone over the dark prairie, the winds were still, and softly Pa played his fiddle.

He let a last note quiver far, far away, until it dissolved in the moonlight. Everything was so beautiful that Laura wanted it to stay so for ever. But Pa said it was time for little girls to go to bed.

Then Laura heard a strange, low, distant sound. 'What's that?' she said.

Pa listened. 'Cattle, by George!' he said. 'Must be the cattle herds going north to Fort Dodge.'

After she was undressed, Laura stood in her nightgown at the window. The air was very still, not a grass blade rustled, and far away and faint she could hear that sound. It was almost a rumble and almost a song.

'Is that singing, Pa?' she asked.

'Yes,' Pa said. 'The cowboys are singing the cattle to sleep. Now hop into bed, you little scallawag!'

Laura thought of cattle lying on the dark ground in the moonlight, and of cowboys softly singing lullabies.

Next morning when she ran out of the house two strange men were sitting on horses by the stable. They were talking to Pa. They were as red-brown as Indians, but their eyes were narrow slits between squinting eyelids. They wore flaps of leather over their legs, and spurs, and wide-brimmed hats. Handkerchiefs were knotted around their necks, and pistols were on their hips.

They said, 'So long,' to Pa, and 'Hi! Yip!' to their horses, and they galloped away.

'Here's a piece of luck!' Pa said to Ma. Those men were cowboys. They wanted Pa to help them keep the cattle out of the ravines among the bluffs of the creek bottoms. Pa would not charge them any money, but he told them he would take a piece of beef. 'How would you like a good piece of beef?' Pa asked.

'Oh, Charles!' said Ma, and her eyes shone.

Pa tied his biggest handkerchief around his neck. He showed Laura how he could pull it up over his mouth and nose to keep the dust out. Then he rode Patty west along the Indian trail, till Laura and Mary couldn't see him any more.

All day the hot sun blazed and the hot winds blew, and the sound of the cattle herds came nearer. It was a faint, mournful sound of cattle lowing. At noon dust was blowing along the horizon. Ma said that so many cattle trampled the grasses flat and stirred up dust from the prairie.

Pa came riding home at sunset, covered with dust. There was dust in his beard and in his hair and on the rims of his eyelids, and dust fell off his clothes. He did not bring any beef, because the cattle were not across the creek yet. The cattle went very slowly, eating grass as they went. They had to eat enough grass to be fat when they came to the cities where people ate them.

Pa did not talk much that night, and he didn't play the fiddle. He went to bed soon after supper.

The herds were so near now that Laura could hear them plainly. The mournful lowing sounded over the prairie till the night was dark. Then the cattle were quieter and the cowboys began to sing. Their songs were not like lullabies. They were high, lonely, wailing songs, almost like the howling of wolves.

Laura lay awake, listening to the lonely songs wandering in the night. Farther away, real wolves howled. Sometimes the cattle lowed. But the cowboys' songs went on, rising and falling and wailing away under the moon. When everyone else was asleep, Laura stole softly to the window, and she saw three fires gleaming like red eyes from the dark edge of the land. Overhead the sky was big and still and full of moonlight. The lonely songs seemed to be crying for the moon. They made Laura's throat ache.

All next day Laura and Mary watched the west. They could hear the far-away bawling of the cattle, they could see dust blowing. Sometimes they thinly heard a shrill yell.

Suddenly a dozen long-horned cattle burst out of the prairie, not far from the stable. They had come up out of a draw going down to the creek bottoms. Their tails stood up and their fierce horns tossed and their feet pounded the ground. A cowboy on a spotted mustang galloped madly to get in front of them. He waved his big hat and yelled sharp, high yells. 'Hi! Yi-yi-yi! Hi? The cattle wheeled, clashing their long horns together. With lifted tails they galloped lumbering away, and behind them the mustang ran and whirled and ran, herding them together. They all went over a rise of ground and down out of sight.

Laura ran back and forth, waving her sun-bonnet and yelling, 'Hi! Yi-yi-yi!' till Ma told her to stop. It was not ladylike to yell like that. Laura wished she could be a cowboy.

Late that afternoon three riders came out of the west, driving one lone cow. One of the riders was Pa, on Patty. Slowly they came nearer, and Laura saw that with the cow was a little spotted calf.

The cow came lunging and plunging. Two cowboys rode well apart in front of her. Two ropes around her long horns were fastened to the cowboys' saddles. When the cow lunged with her horns towards either cowboy the other cowboys pony braced its feet and held her. The cow bawled and the little calf bleated thinner bawls.

Ma watched from the window, while Mary and Laura stood against the house and stared.

The cowboys held the cow with their ropes while Pa tied her to the stable. Then they said good-bye to him and rode away.

Ma could not believe that Pa had actually brought home a cow. But it really was their own cow. The calf was too small to travel, Pa said, and the cow would be too thin to sell, so the cowboys had given them to Pa. They had given him the beef, too; a big chunk was tied to his saddle-horn.

Pa and Ma and Mary and Laura and even Baby Carrie laughed for joy. Pa always laughed out loud and his laugh was like great bells ringing. When Ma was pleased she smiled a gentle smile that made Laura feel warm all over. But now she was laughing because they had a cow.

'Give me a bucket, Caroline,' said Pa. He was going to milk the cow, right away.

He took the bucket, he pushed back his hat, and he squatted by the cow to milk her. And that cow hunched herself and kicked Pa flat on his back.

Pa jumped up. His face was blazing red and his eyes snapped blue sparks.

'Now, by the Great Horn Spoon, I'll milk her!' he said.

He got his axe and he sharpened two stout slabs of oak. He pushed the cow against the stable, and he drove those slabs deep into the ground beside her. The cow bawled and the little calf squalled. Pa tied poles firmly to the posts and stuck their ends into the cracks of the stable, to make a fence.

Now the cow could not move forward nor backward nor sideways. But the little calf could nudge its way between its mother and the stable. So the baby calf felt safe and stopped bawling. It stood on that side of the cow and drank its supper, and Pa put his hand through the fence and milked from the other side. He got a tin cup almost full of milk.

'We'll try again in the morning,' he said. 'The poor thing's as wild as a deer. But we'll gentle her, we'll gentle her.'

The dark was coming on. Nighthawks were chasing insects in the dark air. Bullfrogs were croaking in the creek bottoms. A bud called, 'Whip! Whip! Whip-poor-Will!'

'Who? Who-Oo?' said an owl. Far away the wolves howled, and Jack was growling.

'The wolves are following the herds,' Pa said. 'Tomorrow I'll build a strong high yard for the cow, that wolves can't get into.'

So they all went into the house with the beef. Pa and Ma and Mary and Laura all agreed to give the milk to Baby Carrie. They watched her drink it. The tin cup hid her face, but Laura could see the gulps of milk going down her throat. Gulp by gulp, she swallowed all that good milk. Then she licked the foam from her lips with her red tongue, and laughed.

It seemed a long time before the cornbread and the sizzling beef steaks were done. But nothing had ever tasted so good as that tough, juicy beef. And everyone was happy because now there would be milk to drink, and perhaps even butter for the cornbread.

The lowing of the cattle herds was far away again, and the songs of the cowboys were almost too faint to be heard. All those cattle were on the other side of the creek bottoms now, in Kansas. Tomorrow they would slowly go farther on their long way northward to Fort Dodge, where the soldiers were.

14

Indian Camp

Day after day was hotter than the day before. The wind was hot. 'As if it came out of an oven,' Ma said.

The grass was turning yellow. The whole world was rippling green and gold under the blazing sky.

At noon the wind died. No birds sang. Everything was so still that Laura could hear the squirrels chattering in the trees down by the creek. Suddenly black crows flew overhead, cawing their rough, sharp caws. Then everything was still again.

Ma said that this was midsummer.

Pa wondered where the Indians had gone. He said they had left their little camp on the prairie. And one day he asked Laura and Mary if they would like to see that camp.

Laura jumped up and down and clapped her hands, but Ma objected.

'It is so far, Charles,' she said. 'And in this heat.'

Pa's blue eyes twinkled. 'This heat doesn't hurt the Indians and it won't hurt us,' he said. 'Come on, girls!'

'Please, can't Jack come, too?' Laura begged. Pa had taken his gun, but he looked at Laura and he looked at Jack, then he looked at Ma, and he put the gun up on its pegs again.

'All right, Laura,' he said. 'I'll take Jack, Caroline, and leave you the gun.'

Jack jumped around them, wagging his stump of a tail. As soon as he saw which way they were going, he set off, trotting ahead. Pa came next, and behind him came Mary, and then Laura. Mary kept her sun-bonnet on, but Laura let hers dangle down her back.

The ground was hot under their bare feet. The sunshine pierced through their faded dresses and tingled on their arms and backs. The air was really as hot as the air in an oven, and it smelled faintly like baking bread. Pa said the smell came from all the grass seeds parching in the heat.

They went farther and farther into the vast prairie. Laura felt smaller and smaller. Even Pa did not seem as big as he really was. At last they went down into the little hollow where the Indians had camped.

Jack started up a big rabbit. When it bounded out of the grass Laura jumped. Pa said quickly: 'Let him go, Jack! We have meat enough.' So Jack sat down and watched the big rabbit go bounding away down the hollow.

Laura and Mary looked around them. They stayed close to Pa. Low bushes grew on the sides of the hollow—buckbrush with sprays of berries faintly pink, and sumac holding up green cones but showing here and there a bright red leaf. The goldenrod's plumes were turning grey, and the ox-eyed daisies' yellow petals hung down from the crown centres.

All this was hidden in the secret little hollow. From the house Laura had seen nothing but grasses, and now from this hollow she could not see the house. The prairie seemed to be level, but it was not level.

Laura asked Pa if there were lots of hollows on the prairie, like this one. He said there were.

'Are Indians in them?' she almost whispered. He said he didn't know. There might be.

She held tight to his hand and Mary held to his other hand, and they looked at the Indians' camp. There were ashes where Indian camp fires had been. There were holes in the ground where tent-poles had been driven. Bones were scattered where Indian dogs had gnawed them. All along the sides of the hollow, Indian ponies had bitten the grasses short.

Tracks of big moccasins and smaller moccasins were everywhere, and tracks of little bare toes. And over these tracks were tracks of rabbits and tracks of birds, and wolves' tracks.

Pa read the tracks for Mary and Laura. He showed them tracks of two middle-sized moccasins by the edge of a camp fire's ashes. An Indian woman had squatted there. She wore a leather skirt with fringes; the tiny marks of the fringe were in the dust. The track of her toes inside the moccasins was deeper than the track of her heels, because she had leaned forward to stir something cooking in a pot on the fire.

Then Pa picked up a smoke-blackened forked stick. And he said that the pot had hung from a stick laid across the top of two upright, forked sticks. He showed Mary and Laura the holes where the forked sticks had been driven into the ground. Then he told them to look at the bones around that camp fire and tell him what had cooked in that pot.

They looked, and they said, 'Rabbit.' That was right; the bones were rabbits' bones.

Suddenly Laura shouted, 'Look! Look!' Something bright blue glittered in the dust. She picked it up, and it was a beautiful blue bead. Laura shouted with joy.

Then Mary saw a red bead, and Laura saw a green one, and they forgot everything but beads. Pa helped them look. They found white beads and brown beads, and more and more red and blue beads. All that afternoon they hunted for beads in the dust of the Indian camp. Now and then Pa walked up to the edge of the hollow and looked towards home, then he came back and helped to hunt for more beads. They looked all the ground over carefully.

When they couldn't find any more, it was almost sunset. Laura had a handful of beads, and so did Mary. Pa tied them carefully in his handkerchief, Laura's beads in one corner and Mary's in another corner. He put the handkerchief in his pocket, and they started home.

The sun was low behind their backs when they came out of the hollow. Home was small and very far away. And Pa did not have his gun.

Pa walked so swiftly that Laura could hardly keep up. She trotted as fast as she could, but the sun sank faster. Home seemed farther and farther away. The prairie seemed larger, and a wind ran over it, whispering something frightening. All the grasses shook as if they were scared.

Then Pa turned around and his blue eyes twinkled at Laura. He said: 'Getting tired, little half-pint? It's a long way for little legs.'

He picked her up, big girl that she was, and he settled her safe against his shoulder. He took Mary by the hand, and so they all came home together.

Supper was cooking on the fire, Ma was setting the table, and Baby Carrie played with little pieces of wood on the floor. Pa tossed the handkerchief to Ma.

'I'm later than I meant, Caroline,' he said. 'But look what the girls found.' He took the milk-bucket and went quickly to bring Pet and Patty from their picket-lines and to milk the cow.

Ma untied the handkerchief and exclaimed at what she found. The beads were even prettier than they had been in the Indian camp.

Laura stirred her beads with her finger and watched them sparkle and shine. 'These are mine,' she said.

Then Mary said, 'Carrie can have mine.'

Ma waited to hear what Laura would say. Laura didn't want to say anything. She wanted to keep those pretty beads. Her chest felt all hot inside, and she wished with all her might that Mary wouldn't always be such a good little girl. But she couldn't let Mary be better than she was.

So she said, slowly, 'Carrie can have mine, too.'

'That's my unselfish, good little girls,' said Ma.

She poured Mary's beads into Mary's hands, and Laura's into Laura's hands, and she said she would give them a thread to string them on. The beads would make a pretty necklace for Carrie to wear around her neck.

Mary and Laura sat side by side on their bed, and they strung those pretty beads on the thread that Ma gave them. Each wet her end of the thread in her mouth and twisted it tightly. Then Mary put her end of the thread through the small hole in each of the beads, and Laura put her end through her beads, one by one.

They didn't say anything. Perhaps Mary felt sweet and good inside, but Laura didn't. When she looked at Mary she wanted to slap her. So she dared not look at Mary again.

The beads made a beautiful string. Carrie clapped her hands and laughed when she saw it. Then Ma tied it around Carrie's little neck, and it glittered there. Laura felt a little bit better. After all, her beads were not enough beads to make a whole string, and neither were Mary's, but together they made a whole string of beads for Carrie.

When Carrie felt the beads on her neck, she grabbed at them. She was so little that she did not know any better than to break the string. So Ma untied it, and she put the beads away until Carrie should be old enough to wear them. And often after that Laura thought of those pretty beads and she was still naughty enough to want her beads for herself.

But it had been a wonderful day. She could always think about that long walk across the prairie, and about all they had seen in the Indian camp.

15

Fever 'n' Ague

Now blackberries were ripe, and in the hot afternoons Laura went with Ma to pick them.

The big, black, juicy berries hung thick in brier-patches in the creek bottoms. Some were in the shade of trees and some were in the sun, but the sun was so hot that Laura and Ma stayed in the shade. There were plenty of berries.

Deer lay in the shady groves and watched Ma and Laura. Blue jays flew at their sun-bonnets and scolded because they were taking the berries. Snakes hurriedly crawled away from them, and in the trees the squirrels woke up and chattered at them. Wherever they went among the scratchy briers, mosquitoes rose up in buzzing swarms.

Mosquitoes were thick on the big, ripe berries, sucking the sweet juice. But they liked to bite Laura and Ma as much as they liked to eat blackberries.

Laura's fingers and her mouth were purple-black with berry juice. Her face and her hands and her bare feet were covered with brier scratches and mosquito bites. And they were spattered with purple stains, too, where she had slapped at the mosquitoes. But every day they brought home pails full of berries, and Ma spread them in the sun to dry.

Every day they ate all the blackberries they wanted, and next winter they would have dried blackberries to stew.

Mary hardly ever went to pick blackberries. She stayed in the house to mind Baby Carrie, because she was older. In the daytime there were only one or two mosquitoes in the house. But at night, if the wind wasn't blowing hard, mosquitoes came in thick swarms. On still nights Pa kept piles of damp grass burning all around the house and the stable. The damp grass made a smudge of smoke, to keep the mosquitoes away. But a good many mosquitoes came, anyway.

Pa could not play his fiddle in the evenings because so many mosquitoes bit him. Mr Edwards did not come visiting after supper any more, because the mosquitoes were so thick in the bottoms. All night Pet and Patty and the colt and the calf and the cow were stamping and swishing their tails in the stable. And in the morning Laura's forehead was speckled with mosquito bites.

'This won't last long,' Pa said. 'Fall's not far away, and the first cold wind will settle 'em!'

Laura did not feel very well. One day she felt cold even in the hot sunshine, and she could not get warm by the fire.

Ma asked why she and Mary did not go out to play, and Laura said she didn't feel like playing. She was tired and she ached. Ma stopped her work and asked, 'Where do you ache?'

Laura didn't exactly know. She said: 'I just ache. My legs ache.'

'I ache, too,' Mary said.

Ma looked at them and said they looked healthy enough. But she said something must be wrong or they wouldn't be so quiet. She pulled up Laura's skirt and petticoats to see where her legs ached, and suddenly Laura shivered all over. She shivered so that her teeth rattled in her mouth.

Ma put her hand against Laura's cheek. 'You can't be cold,' she said. 'Your face is hot as fire.'

Laura felt like crying, but of course she didn't. Only little babies cried. 'I'm hot now,' she said. 'And my back aches.'

Ma called Pa, and he came in. 'Charles, do look at the girls,' she said. 'I do believe they are sick.'

'Well, I don't feel any too well myself,' said Pa. 'First I'm hot and then I'm cold, and I ache all over. Is that the way you feel, girls? Do your very bones ache?'

Mary and Laura said that was the way they felt. Then Ma and Pa looked a long time at each other and Ma said, 'The place for you girls is bed.'

It was so queer to be put to bed in the daytime, and Laura was so hot that everything seemed wavering. She held on to Ma's neck while Ma was undressing her, and she begged Ma to tell her what was wrong with her.

'You will be all right. Don't worry,' Ma said, cheerfully. Laura crawled into bed and Ma tucked her in.. It felt good to be in bed. Ma smoothed her forehead with her cool, soft hand and said, 'There, now. Go to sleep.'

Laura did not exactly go to sleep, but she didn't really wake up again for a long, long time. Strange things seemed to keep happening in a haze. She would see Pa crouching by the fire in the middle of the night, then suddenly sunshine hurt her eyes and Ma fed her broth from a spoon. Something dwindled slowly, smaller and smaller, till it was tinier than the tiniest thing. Then slowly it swelled till it was larger than anything could be. Two voices jabbered faster and faster, then a slow voice drawled more slowly than Laura could bear. There were no words, only voices.

Mary was hot in the bed beside her. Mary threw off the covers, and Laura cried because she was so cold. Then she was burning up, and Pa's hand shook the cup of water. Water spilled down her neck. The tin cup rattled against her teeth till she could hardly drink. Then Ma tucked in the covers and Ma's hand burned against Laura's cheek.

She heard Pa say, 'Go to bed, Caroline.'

Ma said, 'You're sicker than I am, Charles.'

Laura opened her eyes and saw bright sunshine. Mary was

sobbing, 'I want a drink of water! I want a drink of water! I want a drink of water!' Jack went back and forth between the big bed and the little bed. Laura saw Pa lying on the floor by the big bed.

Jack pawed at Pa and whined. He took hold of Pa's sleeve with his teeth and shook it. Pa's head lifted up a little and he said, 'I must get up, I must. Caroline and the girls.' Then his head fell back and he lay still. Jack lifted up his nose and howled.

Laura tried to get up, but she was too tired. Then she saw Ma's red face looking over the edge of the big bed. Mary was all the time crying for water. Ma looked at Mary and then she looked at Laura, and she whispered, 'Laura, can you?'

'Yes, Ma,' Laura said. This time she got out of bed. But when she tried to stand up, the floor rocked and she fell down. Jack's tongue lapped and lapped at her face, and he quivered and whined. But he stood still and firm when she took hold of him and sat up against him.

She knew she must get water to stop Mary's crying, and she did. She crawled all the way across the floor to the water-bucket. There was only a little water in it.

She shook so with cold that she could hardly get hold of the dipper. But she did get hold of it. She dipped up some water, and she set out to cross that enormous floor again. Jack stayed beside her all the way.

Mary's eyes didn't open. Her hands held on to the dipper and her mouth swallowed all the water out of it. Then she stopped crying. The dipper fell on the floor, and Laura crawled under the covers. It was a long time before she began to get warm again.

Sometimes she heard Jack sobbing. Sometimes he howled and she thought he was a wolf, but she was not afraid. She lay burning up and hearing him howl. She heard the voices jabbering again, and the slow voice drawling, and she opened her eyes and saw a big, black face close above her face.

It was coal-black and shiny. Its eyes were black and soft. Its teeth shone white in a thick, big mouth. This face smiled, and a deep voice said, softly, 'Drink this, little girl.'

An arm lifted under her shoulders, and a black hand held a cup to her mouth. Laura swallowed a bitter swallow and tried to turn her head away, but the cup followed her mouth. The mellow, deep voice said again, 'Drink it. It will make you well.' So Laura swallowed the whole bitter dose.

When she woke up, a fat woman was stirring the fire. Laura looked at her carefully and she was not black. She was tanned, like Ma.

'I want a drink of water, please,' Laura said.

The fat woman brought it at once. The good, cold water made Laura feel better. She looked at Mary asleep beside her; she looked at Pa and Ma asleep in the big bed. Jack lay half asleep on the floor. Laura looked again at the fat woman and asked, 'Who are you?'

'I'm Mrs Scott,' the woman said, smiling. 'There now, you feel better, don't you?'

'Yes, thank you,' Laura said politely. The fat woman brought her a cup of hot prairie-chicken broth.

'Drink it all up, like a good child,' she said. Laura drank every drop of the good broth. 'Now go to sleep,' said Mrs Scott. 'I'm here to take care of everything till you're all well.'

Next morning Laura felt so much better that she wanted to get up, but Mrs Scott said she must stay in bed until the doctor came. She lay and watched Mrs Scott tidy the house and give medicine to Pa and Ma and Mary. Then it was Laura's turn. She opened her mouth, and Mrs Scott poured a dreadful bitterness out of a small folded paper on to Laura's tongue. Laura drank water and swallowed and swallowed and drank again. She could swallow the powder but she couldn't swallow the bitterness.

Then the doctor came. And he was the black man. Laura had never seen a black man before and she could not take her eyes off Dr Tan. He was so very black. She would have been afraid of him if she had not liked him so much. He smiled at her with all his white teeth. He talked with Pa and Ma, and laughed a rolling, jolly laugh. They all wanted him to stay longer, but he had to hurry away.

Mrs Scott said that all the settlers, up and down the creek, had fever 'n' ague. There were not enough well people to take care of the sick, and she had been going from house to house, working night and day.

'It's a wonder you ever lived through,' she said. 'All of you down at once.' What might have happened if Dr Tan hadn't found them, she didn't know.

Dr Tan was a doctor with the Indians. He was on his way north to Independence when he came to Pa's house. It was a strange thing that Jack, who hated strangers and never let one come near the house until Pa or Ma told him to, had gone to meet Dr Tan and begged him to come in.

'And here you all were, more dead than alive,' Mrs Scott said. Dr Tan had stayed with them a day and a night before Mrs Scott came. Now he was doctoring all the sick settlers.

Mrs Scott said that all this sickness came from eating water-melons. She said, 'I've said a hundred times, if I have once, that water-melons—'

'What's that?' Pa exclaimed. 'Who's got water-melons?'

Mrs Scott said that one of the settlers had planted water-melons in the creek bottoms. And every soul who had eaten one of those melons was down sick that very minute. She said she had warned them. 'But, no,' she said. 'There was no arguing with them. They would eat those melons, and now they're paying for it.'

'I haven't tasted a good slice of water-melon since Hector was a pup,' said Pa.

Next day he was out of bed. The next day, Laura was up. Then Ma got up, and then Mary. They were all thin and shaky, but they could take care of themselves. So Mrs Scott went home.

Ma said she didn't know how they could ever thank her, and Mrs Scott said, 'Pshaw! What are neighbours for but to help each other out?'

Pa's cheeks were hollows and he walked slowly. Ma often sat down to rest. Laura and Mary didn't feel like playing. Every morning they all took those bitter powders. But Ma still smiled her lovely smile, and Pa whistled cheerfully.

'It's an ill wind that doesn't blow some good,' he said. He wasn't able to work, so he could make a rocking-chair for Ma.

He brought some slender willows from the creek bottoms, and he made the chair in the house. He could stop any time to put wood on the fire or lift a kettle for Ma.

First he made four stout legs and braced them firmly with cross-pieces. Then he cut thin strips of the tough willow-skin, just under the bark. He wove these strips back and forth, under and over, till they made a seat for the chair.

He split a long, straight sapling down the middle. He pegged one end of half of it to the side of the seat, and curved it up and over and down, and pegged the other end to the other side of the seat. That made a high, curved back to the chair. He braced it firmly, and then he wove the thin willow-strips across and up and down, under and over each other, till they filled in the chairback.

With the other half of the split sapling Pa made arms for the chair. He curved them from the front of the seat to the chair-back, and he filled them in with woven strips.

Last of all, he split a larger willow which had grown in a curve. He turned the chair upside down, and he pegged the curved pieces to its legs, to make the rockers. And the chair was done.

Then they made a celebration. Ma took of her apron and smoothed her smooth brown hair. She pinned her gold pin in the front of her collar. Mary tied the string of beads around Carrie's neck. Pa and Laura put Mary's pillow on the chair-seat, and set Laura's pillow against its back. Over the pillows Pa spread the quilt from the little bed. Then he took Ma's hand and led her to the chair, and he put Baby Carrie in her arms.

Ma leaned back in the softness. Her thin cheeks flushed and her eyes sparkled with tears, but her smile was beautiful. The chair rocked her gently and she said, 'Oh, Charles! I haven't been so comfortable since I don't know when.'

Then Pa took his fiddle, and he played and sang to Ma in the firelight. Ma rocked and Baby Carrie went to sleep, and Mary and Laura sat on their bench and were happy.

The very next day, without saying where he was going, Pa rode away on Patty. Ma wondered and wondered where he had gone. And when Pa came back he was balancing a water-melon in front of him on the saddle.

He could hardly carry it into the house. He let it fall on the floor, and dropped down beside it.

'I thought I'd never get it here,' he said. 'It must weigh forty pounds, and I'm as weak as water. Hand me the butcher knife.'

'But, Charles!' Ma said. 'You mustn't. Mrs Scott said—'

Pa laughed his big, pealing laugh again. 'But that's not reasonable,' he said. 'This is a good melon. Why should it have fever 'n' ague? Everybody knows that fever 'n' ague comes from breathing the night air.'

'This water-melon grew in the night air,' said Ma.

'Nonsense!' Pa said. 'Give me the butcher knife. I'd eat this melon if I knew it would give me chills and fever.'

'I do believe you would,' said Ma, handing him the knife.

It went into the melon with a luscious sound. The green rind split open, and there was the bright red inside, flecked with black seeds. The red heart actually looked frosty. Nothing had ever been so tempting as that watermelon, on that hot day.

Ma would not taste it. She would not let Laura and Mary eat one bite. But Pa ate slice after slice after slice, until at last he sighed and said the cow could have the rest of it.

Next day he had a little chill and a little fever. Ma blamed the water-melon. But next day she had a chill and a little fever. So, they did not know what could have caused their fever 'n' ague.

No one knew, in those days, that fever 'n' ague was malaria, and that some mosquitoes give it to people when they bite them.

16

Fire in the Chimney

The prairie had changed. Now it was a dark yellow, almost brown, and red streaks of sumac lay across it. The wind wailed in the tall grass, and it whispered sadly across the curly, short buffalo grass. At night the wind sounded like someone crying.

Pa said again that this was a great country. In the Big Woods he had had to cut hay and cure it and stack it and put it in the barn for winter. Here on the High Prairie, the sun had cured the wild grass where it stood, and all winter the mustangs and the cow could mow their own hay. He needed only a small stack, for stormy days.

Now the weather was cooler and he would go to town. He had not gone while the summer was hot, because the heat would be too hard on Pet and Patty. They must pull the wagon twenty miles a day, to get to town in two days. And he did not want to be away from home any longer than he had to.

He stacked the small stack of hay by the barn. He cut the winter's wood and corded it in a long cord against the house. Now he had only to get meat enough to last while he was gone, so he took his gun and went hunting.

Laura and Mary played in the wind outdoors. When they heard a shot echo in the woods along the creek, they knew that Pa had got some meat.

The wind was cooler now, and all along the creek bottoms flocks of wild ducks were rising, flying, settling again.

Up from the creek came long lines of wild geese, forming in V's for their flight farther south. The leader in front called to those behind him. 'Honk?' he called. All down the lines the wild geese answered, one after another. 'Honk.' 'Honk'. 'Honk'. Then he cried, 'Honk!' And, 'Honk-honk ! Honk-honk!' the others answered him. Straight away south he flew on his strong wings, and the long lines evenly followed him.

The tree-tops along the creek were coloured now. Oaks were reds and yellows and browns and greens. Cottonwoods and sycamores and walnuts were sunshiny yellow. The sky was not so brightly blue, and the wind was rough.

That afternoon the wind blew fiercely and it was cold. Ma called Mary and Laura into the house. She built up the fire and drew her rocker near it, and she sat rocking Baby Carrie and singing softly to her:

> 'By lo, baby bunting.
> Papa's gone a-hunting,
> To get a rabbit skin
> To wrap the baby bunting in.'

Laura heard a little crackling in the chimney. Ma stopped singing. She bent forward and looked up the chimney. Then she got up quietly, put Carrie in Mary's arms, pushed Mary down into the rocking-chair, and hurried outdoors. Laura ran after her.

The whole top of the chimney was on fire. The sticks that made it were burning up. The fire was roaring in the wind and licking towards the helpless roof. Ma seized a long pole and struck and struck at the roaring fire, and burning sticks fell all around her.

Laura didn't know what to do. She grabbed a pole, too, but Ma told her to stay away. The roaring fire was terrible.

It could burn the whole house and Laura couldn't do anything.

She ran into the house. Burning sticks and coals were falling down the chimney and rolling out on the hearth. The house was full of smoke. One big, blazing stick rolled on the floor, under Mary's skirts. Mary couldn't move, she was so scared.

Laura was too scared to think. She grabbed the back of the heavy rocking-chair and pulled with all her might. The chair with Mary and Carrie in it came sliding back across the floor. Laura grabbed up the burning stick and flung it into the fireplace just as Ma came in.

'That's a good girl, Laura, to remember I told you never to leave fire on the floor,' Ma said. She took the water-pail and quickly and quietly poured water on the fire in the fireplace. Clouds of steam came out.

Then Ma said, 'Did you burn your hands?' She looked at Laura's hands, but they were not burned, because she had thrown the burning stick so quickly.

Laura was not really crying. She was too big to cry. Only one tear ran out of each eye and her throat choked up, but that was not crying. She hid her face against Ma and hung on to her tight. She was so glad the fire had not hurt Ma.

'Don't cry, Laura,' Ma said, stroking her hair. 'Were you afraid?'

'Yes,' Laura said. 'I was afraid Mary and Carrie would burn up. I was afraid the house would burn up and we wouldn't have any house. I'm—I'm scared now!'

Mary could talk now. She told Ma how Laura had pulled the chair away from the fire. Laura was so little, and the chair so big and so heavy with Mary and Carrie in it, that Ma was surprised. She said she didn't know how Laura had done it.

'You were a brave girl, Laura,' she said. But Laura had really been terribly scared.

'And no harm's done,' Ma said. 'The house didn't burn

up, and Mary's skirts didn't catch fire and burn her and Carrie. So everything is all right.'

When Pa came home he found the fire out. The wind was roaring over the low stone top of the chimney and the house was cold. But Pa said he would build up the chimney with green sticks and fresh clay, and plaster it so well that it wouldn't catch fire again.

He had brought four fat ducks, and he said he could have killed hundreds. But four were all they needed. He said to Ma, 'You save the feathers from the ducks and geese we eat, and I'll shoot you a feather bed.'

He could, of course, have got a deer, but the weather was not yet cold enough to freeze the meat and keep it from spoiling before they could eat it. And he had found the place where a flock of wild turkeys roosted. 'Our Thanksgiving and Christmas turkeys,' he said. 'Great, big, fat fellows. I'll get them when the time comes.'

Pa went whistling to mix mud and cut green sticks and build the chimney up again, while Ma cleaned the ducks. Then the fire merrily crackled, a fat duck roasted, and the cornbread baked. Everything was snug and cosy again.

After supper Pa said he supposed he'd better start to town early next morning. 'Might as well go and get it over with,' he said.

'Yes, Charles, you'd better go,' Ma said.

'We could get along all right, if I didn't,' said Pa. 'There's no need of running to town all the time, for every little thing. I have smoked better tobacco than that stuff Scott raised back in Indiana, but it will do. I'll raise some next summer and pay him back. I wish I hadn't borrowed those nails from Edwards.'

'You did borrow them, Charles,' Ma replied. 'And as for the tobacco, you don't like borrowing any more than I do. We need more quinine. I've been sparing with the cornmeal, but it's almost gone and so is the sugar. You could find a bee-tree, but there's no cornmeal tree to be found, so far as I know, and we'll raise no corn till next year. A little salt pork would taste good, too, after all this wild game. And, Charles, I'd like to write to the folks in Wisconsin. If you mail a letter now, they can write this winter, and then we can hear from them next spring.'

'You're right, Caroline. You always are,' Pa said. Then he turned to Mary and Laura and said it was bedtime. If he was going to start early in the morning, he'd better start sleeping early tonight.

He pulled off his boots while Mary and Laura got into their nightgowns. But when they were in bed he took down his fiddle. Softly he played and softly sang,

> 'So green grows the laurel,
>   And so does the rue,
> So woeful, my love,
>   At the parting with you.'

Ma turned towards him and smiled. 'Take care of yourself on the trip, Charles, and don't worry about us,' she told him. 'We will be all right.'

17

Pa Goes to Town

Before dawn, Pa went away. When Laura and Mary woke, he was gone and everything was empty and lonely. It was not as though Pa had only gone hunting. He was going to town, and he would not be back for four long days.

Bunny had been shut in the stable, so she couldn't follow her mother. The trip was too long for a colt. Bunny whinnied lonesomely. Laura and Mary stayed in the house with Ma. Outdoors was too large and empty to play in when Pa was away. Jack was uneasy, too, and watchful.

At noon Laura went with Ma to water Bunny and to move the cow's picket-pin to fresh grass. The cow was quite gentle now. She followed where Ma led, and she would even let Ma milk her.

At milking-time Ma was putting on her bonnet, when suddenly all Jack's hair stood up stiff on his neck and back, and he rushed out of the house. They heard a yell and a scramble and a shout: 'Call off your dog! Call off your dog!'

Mr Edwards was on top of the woodpile, and Jack was climbing up after him.

'He's got me treed,' Mr Edwards said, backing along the top of the woodpile. Ma could hardly make Jack come away. Jack grinned savagely and his eyes were red. He had to let

Mr Edwards come down from the woodpile, but he watched him every minute.

Ma said, 'I declare, he seems to know that Mr Ingalls isn't here.'

Mr Edwards said that dogs knew more than most folks gave them credit for.

On his way to town that morning, Pa had stopped at Mr Edwards' house and asked him to come over every day to see that everything was all right. And Mr Edwards was such a good neighbour that he had come at chore-time, to do the chores for Ma. But Jack had made up his mind not to let anyone but Ma go near the cow or Bunny while Pa was gone. He had to be shut in the house while Mr Edwards did the chores.

When Mr Edwards went away he said to Ma, 'Keep that dog in the house tonight, and you'll be safe enough.'

The dark crept slowly all around the house. The wind cried mournfully and owls said, 'Who-oo? Oo-oo.' A wolf howled, and Jack growled low in his throat. Mary and Laura sat close to Ma in the firelight. They knew they were safe in the house, because Jack was there and Ma had pulled the latch-string in.

Next day was empty like the first. Jack paced around the stable and around the house, then around the stable and back to the house. He would not pay any attention to Laura.

That afternoon Mrs Scott came to visit with Ma. While they visited, Laura and Mary sat politely, as still as mice. Mrs Scott admired the new rocking-chair. The more she rocked in it, the more she enjoyed it, and she said how neat and comfortable and pretty the house was.

She said she hoped to goodness they would have no trouble with Indians. Mr Scott had heard rumours of trouble. She said, 'Land knows, they'd never do anything with this country themselves. All they do is roam around over it like wild animals. Treaties or no treaties, the land belongs to folks that'll farm it. That's only common sense and justice.'

She did not know why the government made treaties with Indians. The only good Indian was a dead Indian. The very thought of Indians made her blood run cold. She said, 'I can't forget the Minnesota massacre. My Pa and my brothers went out with the rest of the settlers, and stopped them only fifteen miles west of us. I've heard Pa tell often enough how they—'

Ma made a sharp sound in her throat, and Mrs Scott stopped. Whatever a massacre was, it was something that grown-ups would not talk about when little girls were listening.

After Mrs Scott had gone, Laura asked Ma what a massacre was. Ma said she could not explain that now; it was something that Laura would understand when she was older.

Mr Edwards came to do the chores again that evening, and again Jack treed him on the woodpile. Ma had to drag him off. She told Mr Edwards she couldn't think what had got into that dog. Maybe it was the wind that upset him.

The wind had a strange, wild howl in it, and it went through Laura's clothes as if the clothes weren't there. Her teeth and Mary's teeth chattered while they carried many armfuls of wood into the house.

That night they thought of Pa, in Independence. If nothing had delayed him, he would be camping there now, near the houses and the people. Tomorrow he would be in the store, buying things. Then, if he could get an early start, he could come part way home and camp on the prairie tomorrow night. And the next night he might come home.

In the morning the wind was blowing fiercely and it was so cold that Ma kept the door shut. Laura and Mary stayed by the fire and listened to the wind screaming around the house and howling in the chimney. That afternoon they wondered if Pa was leaving Independence and coming towards them, against that wind.

Then, when it was dark, they wondered where he was camping. The wind was bitterly cold. It came even into the snug house and made their backs shiver while their faces roasted in the heat of the fire. Somewhere on the big, dark, lonesome prairie Pa was camping in that wind.

The next day was very long. They could not expect Pa in the morning, but they were waiting till they could expect him. In the afternoon they began to watch the creek road. Jack was watching it, too. He whined to go out, and he went all around the stable and the house, stopping to look towards the creek bottoms and show his teeth. The wind almost blew him off his feet.

When he came in he would not lie down. He walked about, and worried. The hair rose on his neck, and flattened, and rose again. He tried to look out of the window, and then whined at the door. But when Ma opened it, he changed his mind and would not go out.

'Jack's afraid of something,' Mary said.

'Jack's not afraid of anything, ever!' Laura contradicted.

'Laura, Laura,' Ma said. 'It isn't nice to contradict.'

In a minute Jack decided to go out. He went to see that the cow and calf and Bunny were safe in the stable. And Laura wanted to tell Mary, 'I told you so!' She didn't, but she wanted to.

At chore-time Ma kept Jack in the house so he could not tree Mr Edwards on the woodpile. Pa had not come yet. The wind blew Mr Edwards in through the door. He was breathless, and stiff with cold. He warmed himself by the fire before he did the chores, and when he had done them he sat down to warm himself again.

He told Ma that Indians were camping in the shelter of the bluffs. He had seen the smoke from their fires when he crossed the bottoms. He asked Ma if she had a gun.

Ma said she had Pa's pistol, and Mr Edwards said, 'I reckon they'll stay close in camp, a night like this.'

'Yes,' Ma said.

Mr Edwards said he could make himself right comfortable with hay in the stable, and he would spend the night there if Ma said so. Ma thanked him nicely, but said she would not put him to that trouble. They would be safe enough with Jack.

'I am expecting Mr Ingalls any minute now,' she told him. So Mr Edwards put on his coat and cap and muffler and mittens and picked up his gun. He said he didn't guess that anything would bother her, anyway.

'No,' Ma said.

When she shut the door behind him, she pulled the latch-string in, though darkness had not yet come. Laura and Mary could see the creek road plainly, and they watched it until the dark hid it. Then Ma closed and barred the wooden window shutter. Pa had not come.

They ate supper. They washed the dishes and swept the hearth, and still he had not come. Out in the dark where he was, the wind shrieked and wailed and howled. It rattled the door-latch and shook the shutters. It screamed down the chimney and the fire roared and flared.

All the time Laura and Mary strained their ears to hear the sound of wagon wheels. They knew Ma was listening, too, though she was rocking and singing Carrie to sleep.

Carrie fell asleep and Ma went on gently rocking. At last she undressed Carrie and put her to bed. Laura and Mary looked at each other; they didn't want to go to bed.

'Bedtime, girls!' Ma said. Then Laura begged to be allowed to sit up till Pa came, and Mary backed her up, till Ma said they might.

For a long, long time they sat up. Mary yawned, then Laura yawned, then they both yawned. But they kept their eyes wide open. Laura's eyes saw things grow very large and then very small, and sometimes she saw two Marys and sometimes she couldn't see at all, but she was going to sit up till Pa came. Suddenly a fearful crash scared her and Ma picked her up. She had fallen off the bench, smack on the floor.

She tried to tell Ma that she wasn't sleepy enough to have to go to bed, but an enormous yawn almost split her head in two.

In the middle of the night she sat straight up. Ma was sitting still in the rocking-chair by the fire. The doorlatch rattled, the shutters shook, the wind was howling. Mary's eyes were open and Jack walked up and down. Then Laura heard again a wild howl that rose and fell and rose again.

'Lie down, Laura, and go to sleep,' Ma said gently.

'What's that howling?' Laura asked.

'The wind is howling,' said Ma. 'Now mind me, Laura.'

Laura lay down, but her eyes would not shut. She knew that Pa was out in the dark, where that terrible howling was. The wild men were in the bluffs along the creek bottoms, and Pa would have to cross the creek bottoms in the dark. Jack growled.

Then Ma began to sway gently in the comfortable rocking-chair. Firelight ran up and down, up and down the barrel of Pa's pistol in her lap. And Ma sang, softly and sweetly

'There is a happy land,
   Far, far away,
Where saints in glory stand,
   Bright, bright as day.

'Oh, to hear the angels sing,
   Glory to the Lord, our King—'

Laura didn't know that she had gone to sleep. She thought the shining angels began to sing with Ma, and she lay listening to their heavenly singing until suddenly her eyes opened and she saw Pa standing by the fire.

She jumped out of bed, shouting, 'Oh Pa! Pa!'

Pa's boots were caked with frozen mud, his nose was red with cold, his hair wildly stood up on his head. He was so cold that coldness came through Laura's nightgown when she reached him.

'Wait!' he said. He wrapped Laura in Ma's big shawl, and then he hugged her. Everything was all right. The house was cosy with firelight, there was the warm, brown smell of coffee, Ma was smiling, and Pa was there.

The shawl was so large that Mary wrapped the other end of it around her. Pa pulled off his stiff boots and warmed his stiff, cold hands. Then he sat on the bench and he took Mary on one knee and Laura on the other and he hugged them against him, all snuggled in the shawl. Their bare toes toasted in the heat from the fire.

'Ah!' Pa sighed. 'I thought I never would get here.'

Ma rummaged among the stores he had brought, and spooned brown sugar into a tin cup. Pa had brought sugar from Independence. 'Your coffee will be ready in a minute, Charles,' she said.

'It rained between here and Independence, going,' Pa told them. 'And coming back, the mud froze between the spokes till the wheels were nearly solid. I had to get out and knock it loose, so the horses could pull the wagon. And seemed like we'd no more than started, when I had to get out and do it again. It was all I could do to keep Pet and Patty coming against that wind. They're so worn out they can hardly stagger. I never saw such a wind; it cuts like a knife.'

The wind had begun while he was in town. People there told him he had better wait until it blew itself out, but he wanted to get home.

'It beats me,' he said, 'why they call a south wind a norther, and how a wind from the south can be so tarnation cold. I never saw anything like it. Down here in this country, the north end of a south wind is the coldest wind I ever heard of.'

He drank his coffee and wiped his moustache with his handkerchief, and said: 'Ah! That hits the spot, Caroline! Now I'm beginning to thaw out.'

Then his eyes twinkled at Ma and he told her to open the square package on the table. 'Be careful,' he said. 'Don't drop it.'

Ma stopped unwrapping it and said: 'Oh, Charles! You didn't!'

'Open it,' Pa said.

In that square package there were eight small squares of window-glass. They would have glass windows in their house.

Not one of the squares was broken. Pa had brought them safely all the way home. Ma shook her head and said he shouldn't have spent so much, but her whole face was smiling and Pa laughed with joy. They were all so pleased. All winter long they could look out of the windows as much as they liked, and the sunshine could come in.

Pa said he thought that Ma and Mary and Laura would like glass windows better than any other present, and he was right. They did. But the windows were not all he had brought them. There was a little paper sack full of pure white sugar. Ma opened it and Mary and Laura looked at the sparkling whiteness of that beautiful sugar, and they each had a taste of it from a spoon. Then Ma tied it carefully up. They would have white sugar when company came.

Best of all, Pa was safely home again.

Laura and Mary went back to sleep, very comfortable all over. Everything was all right when Pa was there. And now he had nails, and cornmeal, and fat pork, and salt, and everything. He would not have to go to town again for a long time.

18

The Tall Indian

In those three days the norther had howled and screeched across the prairie till it blew itself out. Now the sun was warm and the wind was mild, but there was a feeling of autumn in the air.

Indians came riding on the path that passed so close to the house. They went by as though it were not there.

They were thin and brown and bare. They rode their little ponies without saddle or bridle. They sat up straight on the naked ponies and did not look to right or left. But their black eyes glittered.

Laura and Mary backed against the house and looked up at them. And they saw red-brown skin bright against the blue sky, and scalplocks wound with coloured string, and feathers quivering. The Indians' faces were like the red-brown wood that Pa had carved to make a bracket for Ma.

'I thought that trail was an old one they didn't use any more,' Pa said. 'I wouldn't have built the house so close to it if I'd known it's a highroad.'

Jack hated Indians, and Ma said she didn't blame him. She said, 'I declare, Indians are getting so thick around here that I can't look up without seeing one.'

As she spoke she looked up, and there stood an Indian. He stood in the doorway, looking at them, and they had not heard a sound.

'Goodness!' Ma gasped.

Silently Jack jumped at the Indian. Pa caught him by the collar, just in time. The Indian hadn't moved; he stood as still as if Jack hadn't been there at all.

'How!' he said to Pa.

Pa held on to Jack and replied, 'How!' He dragged Jack to the bedpost and tied him there. While he was doing it, the Indian came in and squatted down by the fire.

Then Pa squatted down by the Indian, and they sat there, friendly but not saying a word, while Ma finished cooking dinner.

Laura and Mary were close together and quiet on their bed in the corner. They couldn't take their eyes from that Indian. He was so still that the beautiful eagle-feathers in his scalplock didn't stir. Only his bare chest and the leanness under his ribs moved a little to his breathing. He wore fringed leather leggings, and his moccasins were covered with beads.

Ma gave Pa and the Indian their dinners on two tin plates, and they ate silently. Then Pa gave the Indian some tobacco for his pipe. They filled their pipes, and they lighted the tobacco with coals from the fire, and they silently smoked until the pipes were empty.

All this time nobody had said anything. But now the Indian said something to Pa. Pa shook his head and said, 'No speak.'

A while longer they all sat silent. Then the Indian rose up and went away without a sound.

'My goodness gracious!' Ma said.

Laura and Mary ran to the window. They saw the Indian's straight back, riding away on a pony. He held a gun across his knees, its ends stuck out on either side of him.

Pa said that Indian was no common trash. He guessed by the scalplock that he was an Osage.

'Unless I miss my guess,' Pa said, 'that was French he spoke. I wish I had picked up some of that lingo.'

'Let Indians keep themselves to themselves,' said Ma, 'and

we will do the same. I don't like Indians around underfoot.'

Pa told her not to worry.

'That Indian was perfectly friendly,' he said. 'And their camps down among the bluffs are peaceable enough. If we treat them well and watch Jack, we won't have any trouble.'

The very next morning, when Pa opened the door to go to the stable, Laura saw Jack standing in the Indian trail. He stood stiff, his back bristled, and all his teeth showed. Before him in the path the tall Indian sat on his pony.

Indian and pony were still as still. Jack was telling them plainly that he would spring if they moved. Only the eagle feathers that stood up from the Indian's scalplock were waving and spinning in the wind.

When the Indian saw Pa, he lifted his gun and pointed it straight at Jack.

Laura ran to the door, but Pa was quicker. He stepped between Jack and that gun, and he reached down and grabbed Jack by the collar. He dragged Jack out of the Indian's way, and the Indian rode on, along the trail.

Pa stood with his feet wide apart, his hands in his pockets, and watched the Indian riding farther and farther away across the prairie.

'That was a darned close call!' Pa said. 'Well, it's his path. An Indian trail, long before we came.'

He drove an iron ring into a log of the house wall, and he chained Jack to it. After that, Jack was always chained. He was chained to the house in the daytime, and at night he was chained to the stable door, because horse-thieves were in the country now. They had stolen Mr Edwards' horses.

Jack grew crosser and crosser because he was chained. But it could not be helped. He would not admit that the trail was the Indians' trail, he thought it belonged to Pa.

And Laura knew that something terrible would happen if Jack hurt an Indian.

Winter was coming now. The grasses were a dull colour

under a dull sky. The winds wailed as if they were looking for something they could not find. Wild animals were wearing their thick winter fur, and Pa set his traps in the creek bottoms. Every day he visited them, and ever day he went hunting. Now that the nights were freezing cold, he shot deer for meat. He shot wolves and foxes for their fur, and his traps caught beaver and muskrat and mink.

He stretched the skins on the outside of the house and carefully tacked them there, to dry. In the evenings he worked the dried skins between his hands to make them soft and he added them to the bundle in the corner. Every day the bundle of furs grew bigger.

Laura loved to stroke the thick fur of red foxes. She liked the brown, soft fur of beaver, too, and the shaggy wolf's fur. But best of all she loved the silky mink. Those were all furs that Pa saved to trade next spring in Independence. Laura and Mary had rabbit-skin caps, and Pa's cap was musk-rat.

One day when Pa was hunting, two Indians came. They came into the house, because Jack was chained.

Those Indians were dirty and scowling and mean. They acted as if the house belonged to them. One of them looked through Ma's cupboard and took all the cornbread. The other took Pa's tobacco-pouch. They looked at the pegs where Pa's gun belonged. Then one of them picked up the bundle of furs.

Ma held Baby Carrie in her arms, and Mary and Laura stood close to her. They looked at that Indian taking Pa's furs. They couldn't do anything to stop him.

He carried them as far as the door. Then the other Indian said something to him. They made harsh sounds at each other in their throats, and he dropped the furs. They went away.

Ma sat down. She hugged Mary and Laura close to her and Laura felt Ma's heart beating.

'Well,' Ma said, smiling, 'I'm thankful they didn't take the plough and seeds.'

Laura was surprised. She asked, 'What plough?'

'The plough and all our seeds for next year are in that bundle of furs,' said Ma.

When Pa came home they told him about those Indians, and he looked sober. But he said that all was well that ended well.

That evening when Mary and Laura were in bed, Pa played his fiddle. Ma was rocking in the rocking-chair, holding Baby Carrie against her breast, and she began to sing softly with the fiddle

'Wild roved an Indian maid,
    Bright Alfarata,
Where flow the waters
    Of the blue Juniata.
Strong and true my arrows are
    In my painted quiver,
Swift goes my light canoe
    A-down the rapid river.

'Bold is my warrior good,
    The love of Alfarata,
Proud wave his sunny plumes
    Along the Juniata.
Soft and low he speaks to me,
    And then his war-cry sounding
Rings his voice in thunder loud
    From height to height resounding.

'So sang the Indian maid,
    Bright Alfarata,
Where sweep the waters
    Of the blue Juniata.
Fleeting years have borne away
    The voice of Alfarata,
Still flow the waters
    Of the blue Juniata.'

Ma's voice and the fiddle's music softly died away. And Laura asked, 'Where did the voice of Alfarata go, Ma?'

'Goodness!' Ma said, 'Aren't you asleep yet?'

'I'm going to sleep,' Laura said. 'But please tell me where the voice of Alfarata went?'

'Oh I suppose she went west,' Ma answered. 'That's what the Indians do.'

'Why do they do that, Ma?' Laura asked. 'Why do they go west?'

'They have to,' Ma said.

'Why do they have to?'

'The government makes them, Laura,' said Pa. 'Now go to sleep.'

He played the fiddle softly for a while. Then Laura asked, 'Please, Pa, can I ask just one more question?'

'May I,' said Ma.

Laura began again. 'Pa, please, may I—'

'What is it?' Pa asked. It was not polite for little girls to interrupt, but of course Pa could do it.

'Will the government make these Indians go west?'

'Yes,' Pa said. 'When white settlers come into a country, the Indians have to move on. The government is going to move these Indians farther west, any time now. That's why we're here, Laura. White people are going to settle all this country, and we get the best land because we get here first and take our pick. Now do you understand?'

'Yes, Pa,' Laura said. 'But, Pa, I thought this was Indian Territory. Won't it make the Indians mad to have to—'

'No more questions, Laura,' Pa said, firmly. 'Go to sleep.'

19

Mr Edwards Meets Santa Claus

The days were short and cold, the wind whistled sharply, but there was no snow. Cold rains were falling. Day after day the rain fell, pattering on the roof and pouring from the eaves.

Mary and Laura stayed close by the fire, sewing their nine-patch quilt blocks, or cutting paper dolls from scraps of wrapping-paper, and hearing the wet sound of the rain. Every night was so cold that they expected to see snow next morning, but in the morning they saw only sad, wet grass.

They pressed their noses against the squares of glass in the windows that Pa had made, and they were glad they could see out. But they wished they could see snow.

Laura was anxious because Christmas was near, and Santa Claus and his reindeer could not travel without snow. Mary was afraid that, even if it snowed, Santa Claus could not find them, so far away in Indian Territory. When they asked Ma about this, she said she didn't know.

'What day is it?' they asked her, anxiously. 'How many more days till Christmas?' And they counted off the days on their fingers, till there was only one more day left.

Rain was still falling that morning. There was not one crack in the grey sky. They felt almost sure there would be no Christmas. Still, they kept hoping.

Just before noon the light changed. The clouds broke and drifted apart, shining white in a clear blue sky. The sun shone, birds sang, and thousands of drops of water sparkled on the grasses. But when Ma opened the door to let in the fresh, cold air, they heard the creek roaring.

They had not thought about the creek. Now they knew they would have no Christmas, because Santa Claus could not cross that roaring creek.

Pa came in, bringing a big fat turkey. If it weighed less than twenty pounds, he said, he'd eat it, feathers and all. He asked Laura, 'How's that for a Christmas dinner? Think you can manage one of those drumsticks?'

She said, yes, she could. But she was sober. Then Mary asked him if the creek was going down, and he said it was still rising.

Ma said it was too bad. She hated to think of Mr Edwards eating his bachelor cooking all alone on Christmas day. Mr Edwards had been asked to eat Christmas dinner with them, but Pa shook his head and said a man would risk his neck, trying to cross that creek now.

'No,' he said. 'That current's too strong. We'll just have to make up our minds that Edwards won't be here tomorrow.'

Of course that meant that Santa Claus could not come, either.

Laura and Mary tried not to mind too much. They watched Ma dress the wild turkey, and it was a very fat turkey. They were lucky little girls, to have a good house to live in, and a warm fire to sit by, and such a turkey for their Christmas dinner. Ma said so, and it was true. Ma said it was too bad that Santa Claus couldn't come this year, but they were such good girls that he hadn't forgotten them; he would surely come next year.

Still, they were not happy.

After supper that night they washed their hands and faces,

buttoned their red-flannel nightgowns, tied their nightcap strings, and soberly said their prayers. They lay down in bed and pulled the covers up. It did not seem at all like Christmas time.

Pa and Ma sat silent by the fire. After a while Ma asked why Pa didn't play the fiddle, and he said, 'I don't seem to have the heart to, Caroline.'

After a longer while, Ma suddenly stood up.

'I'm going to hang up your stockings, girls,' she said. 'Maybe something will happen.'

Laura's heart jumped. But then she thought again of the creek and she knew nothing could happen.

Ma took one of Mary's clean stockings and one of Laura's, and she hung them from the mantel-shelf, on either side of the fireplace. Laura and Mary watched her over the edge of their bed-covers.

'Now go to sleep,' Ma said, kissing them good night. 'Morning will come quicker if you're asleep.'

She sat down again by the fire and Laura almost went to sleep. She woke up a little when she heard Pa say, 'You've only made it worse, Caroline.' And she thought she heard Ma say: 'No, Charles. There's the white sugar.' But perhaps she was dreaming.

Then she heard Jack growl savagely. The door-latch rattled and some one said, 'Ingalls! Ingalls!' Pa was stirring up the fire, and when he opened the door Laura saw that it was morning. The outdoors was grey.

'Great fish-hooks, Edwards! Come in, man! What's happened?' Pa exclaimed.

Laura saw the stockings limply dangling, and she scrooged her shut eyes into the pillow. She heard Pa piling wood on the fire, and she heard Mr Edwards say he had carried his clothes on his head when he swam the creek. His teeth rattled and his voice quivered. He would be all right, he said, as soon as he got warm.

'It was too big a risk, Edwards,' Pa said. 'We're glad you're here, but that was too big a risk for a Christmas dinner.'

'Your little ones had to have a Christmas,' Mr Edwards replied. 'No creek could stop me, after I fetched them their gifts from Independence.'

Laura sat straight up in bed. 'Did you see Santa Claus?' she shouted.

'I sure did,' Mr Edwards said.

'Where? When? What did he look like? What did he say? Did he really give you something for us?' Mary and Laura cried.

'Wait, wait a minute!' Mr Edwards laughed. And Ma said she would put the presents in the stockings, as Santa Claus intended. She said they mustn't look.

Mr Edwards came and sat on the floor by their bed, and he answered every question they asked him. They honestly tried not to look at Ma, and they didn't quite see what she was doing.

When he saw the creek rising, Mr Edwards said, he had known that Santa Claus could not get across it. ('But you crossed it,' Laura said. 'Yes,' Mr Edwards replied, 'but Santa Claus is too old and fat. He couldn't make it, where a long, lean razor-back like me could do so.') And Mr Edwards reasoned that if Santa Claus couldn't cross the creek, likely he would come no farther south than Independence. Why should he come forty miles across the prairie, only to be turned back? Of course he wouldn't do that!

So Mr Edwards had walked to Independence. ('In the rain?' Mary asked. Mr Edwards said he wore his rubber coat.) And there, coming down the street in Independence, he had met Santa Claus. ('In the daytime?' Laura asked. She hadn't thought that anyone could see Santa Claus in the daytime. No, Mr Edwards said; it was night, but light shone out across the street from the saloons.)

Well, the first thing Santa Claus said was, 'Hello, Edwards!'

('Did he know you?' Mary asked, and Laura asked, 'How did you know he was really Santa Claus?' Mr Edwards said that Santa Claus knew everybody. And he had recognized Santa at once by his whiskers. Santa Claus had the longest, thickest, whitest set of whiskers west of the Mississippi.)

So Santa Claus said, 'Hello, Edwards! Last time I saw you you were sleeping on a corn-shuck bed in Tennessee.' And Mr Edwards well remembered the little pair of redyarn mittens that Santa Claus had left for him that time.

Then Santa Claus said: 'I understand you're living now down along the Verdigris River. Have you ever met up, down yonder, with two little young girls named Mary and Laura?'

'I surely am acquainted with them,' Mr Edwards replied.

'It rests heavy on my mind,' said Santa Claus. 'They are both of them sweet, pretty, good little young things, and I know they are expecting me. I surely do hate to disappoint two good little girls like them. Yet with the water up the way it is, I can't ever make it across that creek. I can figure no way whatsoever to get to their cabin this year. Edwards, would you do me the favour to fetch them their gifts this one time?'

'I'll do that, and with pleasure,' Mr Edwards told him.

Then Santa Claus and Mr Edwards stepped across the street to the hitching-posts where the pack-mule was tied. ('Didn't he have his reindeer?' Laura asked. 'You know he couldn't,' Mary said. 'There isn't any snow.' 'Exactly,' said Mr Edwards. Santa Claus travelled with a pack-mule in the south-west.)

And Santa Claus uncinched the pack and looked through it, and he took out the presents for Mary and Laura.

'Oh, what are they?' Laura cried; but Mary asked, 'Then what did he do?'

Then he shook hands with Mr Edwards, and he swung up on his fine bay horse. Santa Claus rode well, for a man of his weight and build. And he tucked his long, white whiskers under his bandana. 'So long, Edwards,' he said, and he rode away on the Fort Dodge trail, leading his pack-mule and whistling.

Laura and Mary were silent an instant, thinking of that. Then Ma said, 'You may look now, girls.'

Something was shining bright in the top of Laura' stocking. She squealed and jumped out of bed. So did Mary, but Laura beat her to the fireplace. And the shining thing was a glittering new tin cup.

Mary had one exactly like it.

These new tin cups were their very own. Now they each had a cup to drink out of. Laura jumped up and down and shouted and laughed, but Mary stood still and looked with shining eyes at her own tin cup.

Then they plunged their hands into the stockings again. And they pulled out two long, long sticks of candy. It was peppermint candy, striped red and white. They looked and looked at that beautiful candy, and Laura licked her stick, just one lick. But Mary was not so greedy. She didn't take even one lick of her stick.

Those stockings weren't empty yet. Mary and Laura pulled out two small packages. They unwrapped them, and each found a little heart-shaped cake. Over their delicate brown tops was sprinkled white sugar. The sparkling grains lay like tiny drifts of snow.

The cakes were too pretty to eat. Mary and Laura just looked at them. But at last Laura turned hers over, and she nibbled a tiny nibble from underneath, where it wouldn't show. And the inside of that little cake was white!

It had been made of pure white flour, and sweetened with white sugar.

Laura and Mary never would have looked in their stockings again. The cups and the cakes and the candy were almost too much. They were too happy to speak. But Ma asked if they were sure the stockings were empty.

Then they put their arms down inside them, to make sure.

And in the very toe of each stocking was a shining bright, new penny!

They had never even thought of such a thing as having a penny. Think of having a whole penny for your very own. Think of having a cup and a cake and a stick of candy and a penny.

There never had been such a Christmas.

Now, of course, right away Laura and Mary should have thanked Mr Edwards for bringing those lovely presents all the way from Independence. But they had forgotten all about Mr Edwards. They had even forgotten Santa Claus. In a minute they would have remembered, but before they did, Ma said, gently, 'Aren't you going to thank Mr Edwards?'

'Oh, thank you, Mr Edwards! Thank you!' they said, and they meant it with all their hearts. Pa shook Mr Edwards' hand, too, and shook it again. Pa and Ma and Mr Edwards acted as if they were almost crying, Laura didn't know why. So she gazed again at her beautiful presents.

She looked up again when Ma gasped. And Mr Edwards was taking sweet potatoes out of his pockets. He said they had helped to balance the package on his head when he swam across the creek. He thought Pa and Ma might like them, with the Christmas turkey.

There were nine sweet potatoes. Mr Edwards had brought them all the way from town, too. It was just too much. Pa said so. 'It's too much, Edwards,' he said. They never could thank him enough.

Mary and Laura were much too excited to eat breakfast. They drank the milk from their shining new cups, but they could not swallow the rabbit stew and the cornmeal mush.

'Don't make them, Charles,' Ma said. 'It will soon be dinner-time.'

For Christmas dinner there was the tender, juicy, roasted

turkey. There were the sweet potatoes, baked in the ashes and carefully wiped so that you could eat the good skins, too. There was a loaf of salt-rising bread made from the last of the white flour.

And after all that there were stewed dried blackberries and little cakes. But these little cakes were made with brown sugar and they did not have white sugar sprinkled over their tops.

Then Pa and Ma and Mr Edwards sat by the fire and talked about Christmas times back in Tennessee and up north in the Big Woods. But Mary and Laura looked at their beautiful cakes and played with their pennies and drank water out of their new cups. And little by little they licked and sucked their sticks of candy, till each stick was sharp-pointed on one end.

That was a happy Christmas.

20

A Scream in the Night

The days were short and grey now, the nights were very dark and cold. Clouds hung low above the little house and spread low and far over the bleak prairie. Rain fell, and sometimes snow was driven on the wind. Hard little bits of snow whirled in the air and scurried over the humped backs of miserable grasses. And next day the snow was gone.

Every day Pa went hunting and trapping. In the cosy, fire-lit house Mary and Laura helped Ma with the work. Then they sewed quilt-patches. They played Pat-a-Cake with Carrie, and they played Hide the Thimble. With a piece of string and their fingers, they played Cat's Cradle. And they played Bean Porridge Hot. Facing each other, they clapped their hands together and against each other's hands, keeping time while they said,

> 'Bean porridge hot,
>   Bean porridge cold,
> Bean porridge in the pot,
>   Nine days old.
>
> 'Some like it hot,
>   Some like it cold,
> Some like it in the pot,
>   Nine days old.

'I like it hot,
　　I like it cold,
　　I like it in the pot,
　　　　Nine days old.'

That was true. No supper was so good as the thick bean porridge, flavoured with a small bit of salt pork, that Ma dipped on to the tin plates when Pa had come home cold and tired from his hunting. Laura liked it hot, and she liked it cold, and it was always good as long as it lasted. But it never really lasted nine days. They ate it up before that.

All the time the wind blew, shrieking, howling, wailing, screaming, and mournfully sobbing. They were used to hearing the wind. All day they heard it, and at night in their sleep they knew it was blowing. But one night they heard such a terrible scream that they all woke up.

Pa jumped out of bed, and Ma said: 'Charles! What was it?'

'It's a woman screaming,' Pa said. He was dressing as fast as he could. 'Sounded like it came from Scott's.'

'Oh, what can be wrong!' Ma exclaimed.

Pa was putting on his boots. He put his foot in, and he put his fingers through the strap-ears at the top of the long boot leg. Then he gave a mighty pull, and he stamped hard on the floor, and that boot was on.

'Maybe Scott is sick,' pulling on the other boot.

'You don't suppose—?' Ma asked, low.

'No,' said Pa. 'I keep telling you they won't make any trouble. They're perfectly quiet and peaceable down in those camps among the bluffs.'

Laura began to climb out of bed, but Ma said, 'Lie down and be still, Laura.' So she lay down.

Pa put on his warm, bright plaid coat, and his fur cap, and his muffler. He lighted the candle in the lantern, took his gun, and hurried outdoors.

Before he shut the door behind him, Laura saw the night outside. It was black dark. Not one star was shining. Laura had never seen such solid darkness.

'Ma?' she said.

'What, Laura?'

'What makes it so dark?'

'It's going to storm,' Ma answered. She pulled the latch-string in and put a stick of wood on the fire. Then she went back to bed. 'Go to sleep, Mary and Laura,' she said.

But Ma did not go to sleep, and neither did Mary and Laura. They lay wide awake and listened. They could not hear anything but the wind.

Mary put her head under the quilt and whispered to Laura, 'I wish Pa'd come back.'

Laura nodded her head on the pillow, but she couldn't say anything. She seemed to see Pa striding along the top of the bluff, on the path that went towards Mr Scott's house. Tiny bright spots of candlelight darted here and there from the holes cut in the tin lantern. The little flickering lights seemed to be lost in the black dark.

After a long time Laura whispered, 'It must be 'most morning.' And Mary nodded. All that time they had been lying and listening to the wind, and Pa had not come back.

Then, high above the shrieking of the wind they heard again that terrible scream. It seemed quite close to the house.

Laura screamed, too, and leaped out of bed. Mary ducked under the covers. Ma got up and began to dress in a hurry. She put another stick of wood on the fire and told Laura to go back to bed. But Laura begged so hard that Ma said she could stay up. 'Wrap yourself in the shawl,' Ma said.

They stood by the fire and listened. They couldn't hear anything but the wind. And they could not do anything. But at least they were not lying down in bed.

Suddenly fists pounded on the door and Pa shouted 'Let me in! Quick, Caroline!'

Ma opened the door and Pa slammed it quickly behind him. He was out of breath. He pushed back his cap and said: 'Whew! I'm scared yet.'

'What was it, Charles?' said Ma.

'A panther,' Pa said.

He had hurried as fast as he could go to Mr Scott's. When he got there, the house was dark and everything was quiet. Pa went all around the house, listening, and looking with the lantern. He could not find a sign of anything wrong. So he felt like a fool, to think he had got up and dressed in the middle of the night and walked two miles, all because he heard the wind howl.

He did not want Mr and Mrs Scott to know about it. So he did not wake them up. He came home as fast as he could because the wind was bitter cold. And he was hurrying along the path, where it went on the edge of the bluff, when all of a sudden he heard that scream right under his feet.

'I tell you my hair stood up till it lifted my cap,' he told Laura. 'I lit out for home like a scared rabbit.'

'Where was that panther, Pa?' she asked him.

'In a tree-top,' said Pa. 'In the top of that big cottonwood that grows against the bluff there.'

'Pa, did it come after you?' Laura asked, and he said, 'I don't know, Laura.'

'Well, you're safe now, Charles,' said Ma.

'Yes, and I'm glad of it. This is too dark a night to be out with panthers,' Pa said. 'Now, Laura, where's my bootjack?'

Laura brought it to him. The bootjack was a thin oak slab with a notch in one end and a cleat across the middle of it. Laura laid it on the floor with the cleat down, and the cleat lifted up the notched end. Then Pa stood on it with one foot; he put the other foot into the notch, and the notch held the boot by the heel while Pa pulled his foot out. Then he pulled off his other boot, the same way. The boots clung tightly, but they had to come off.

Laura watched him do this, and then she asked, 'Would a panther carry off a little girl, Pa?'

'Yes,' said Pa. 'And kill her and eat her, too. You and Mary must stay in the house till I shoot that panther. As soon as daylight comes I will take my gun and go after him.'

All the next day Pa hunted that panther. And he hunted the next day and the next day. He found the panther's tracks, and he found the hide and bones of an antelope that the panther had eaten, but he did not find the panther anywhere. The panther went swiftly through tree-tops, where it left no tracks.

Pa said he would not stop till he killed that panther. He said, 'We can't have panthers running around in a country where there are little girls.'

But he did not kill that panther, and he did stop hunting it. One day in the woods he met an Indian. They stood in the wet, cold woods and looked at each other, and they could not talk because they did not know each other's words. But the Indian pointed to the panther's tracks, and he made motions with his gun to show Pa that he had killed that panther. He pointed to the tree-tops and to the ground, to show that he had shot it out of a tree. And he motioned to the sky, and west and east, to say that he had killed it the day before.

So that was all right. The panther was dead.

Laura asked if a panther would carry off a little papoose and kill and eat her, too, and Pa said yes. Probably that was why the Indian had killed that panther.

21

Indian Jamboree

Winter ended at last. There was a softer note in the sound of the wind, and the bitter cold was gone. One day Pa said he had seen a flock of wild geese flying north. It was time to take his furs to Independence.

Ma said, 'The Indians are so near!'

'They are perfectly friendly,' said Pa. He often met Indians in the woods where he was hunting. There was nothing to fear from Indians.

'No,' Ma said. But Laura knew that Ma was afraid of Indians. 'You must go, Charles,' she said. 'We must have a plough and seeds. And you will soon be back again.'

Before dawn next morning Pa hitched Pet and Patty to the wagon, loaded his furs into it, and drove away.

Laura and Mary counted the long, empty days. One, two, three, four, and still Pa had not come home. In the morning of the fifth day they began earnestly to watch for him.

It was a sunny day. There was still a little chill in the wind, but it smelled of spring. The vast blue sky resounded to the quacks of wild ducks and the honk-honk-honking of wild geese. The long, black-dotted lines of them were all flying north.

Laura and Mary played outdoors in the wild, sweet weather. And poor Jack watched them and sighed. He couldn't run and play any more, because he was chained. Laura and Mary tried to comfort him, but he didn't want petting. He wanted to be free again, as he used to be.

Pa didn't come that morning; he didn't come that afternoon. Ma said it must have taken him a long time to trade his furs.

That afternoon Laura and Mary were playing hopscotch. They marked the lines with a stick in the muddy yard. Mary really didn't want to hop; she was almost eight years old and she didn't think that hop-scotch was a ladylike play. But Laura teased and coaxed, and said that if they stayed outdoors they would be sure to see Pa the minute he came from the creek bottoms. So Mary was hopping.

Suddenly she stopped on one foot and said, 'What's that?'

Laura had already heard the queer sound and she was listening to it. She said, 'It's the Indians.'

Mary's other foot dropped and she stood frozen still. She was scared. Laura was not exactly scared, but that sound made her feel funny. It was the sound of quite a lot of Indians, chopping with their voices. It was something like the sound of an axe chopping, and something like a dog barking, and it was something like a song, but not like any song that Laura had ever heard. It was a wild, fierce sound, but it didn't seem angry.

Laura tried to hear it more clearly. She couldn't hear it very well, because hills and trees and the wind were in the way, and Jack was savagely growling.

Ma came outdoors and listened a minute. Then she told Mary and Laura to come into the house. Ma took Jack inside, too, and pulled in the latch-string.

They didn't play any more. They watched at the window, and listened to that sound. It was harder to hear, in the house. Sometimes they couldn't hear it; then they heard it again. It hadn't stopped.

Ma and Laura did the chores earlier than usual. They

locked Bunny and the cow and calf in the stable, and took the milk to the house. Ma strained it and set it away. She drew a bucket of fresh water from the well, while Laura and Mary carried in wood. All the time that sound went on; it was louder, now, and faster. It made Laura's heart beat fast.

They all went into the house and Ma barred the door. The latch-string was already in. They wouldn't go out of the house till morning.

The sun slowly sank. All around the edge of the prairie the edge of the sky flushed pink. Firelight flickered in the dusky house and Ma was getting supper, but Laura and Mary silently watched from the window. They saw the colours fade from everything. The land was shadowy and the sky was clear, pale grey. All the time that sound came from the creek bottoms, louder and louder, faster and faster. And Laura's heart beat faster and louder.

How she shouted when she heard the wagon! She ran to the door and jumped up and down, but she couldn't unbar it. Ma wouldn't let her go out. Ma went out, to help Pa bring in the bundles.

He came in with his arms full, and Laura and Mary clung to his sleeves and jumped on his feet. Pa laughed his jolly big laugh. 'Hey! hey! don't upset me!' he laughed. 'What do you think I am? A tree to climb?'

He dropped the bundles on the table, he hugged Laura in a big bear hug, and tossed her and hugged her again. Then he hugged Mary snugly in his other arm.

'Listen, Pa,' Laura said. 'Listen to the Indians. Why are they making that funny noise?'

'Oh, they're having some kind of jamboree,' Pa said. 'I heard them when I crossed the creek bottoms.'

Then he went out to unhitch the horses and bring in the rest of the bundles. He had got the plough; he left it in the stable, but he brought all the seeds into the house for safety. He had sugar, not any white sugar this time, but brown.

White sugar cost too much. But he had brought a little white flour. There were cornmeal and salt and coffee and all the seeds they needed. Pa had even got seed potatoes. Laura wished they might eat the potatoes but they must be saved to plant.

Then Pa's face beamed and he opened a small paper sack. It was full of crackers. He set it on the table, and he unwrapped and set beside it a glass jar full of little green cucumber pickles.

'I thought we'd all have a treat,' he said.

Laura's mouth watered, and Ma's eyes shone softly at Pa. He had remembered how she longed for pickles.

That wasn't all. He gave Ma a package and watched her unwrap it and in it was enough pretty calico to make her a dress.

'Oh, Charles, you shouldn't! It's too much!' she said. But her face and Pa's were two beams of joy.

Now he hung up his cap and his plaid coat on their pegs. His eyes looked sideways at Laura and Mary, but that was all. He sat down and stretched out his legs to the fire.

Mary sat down, too, and folded her hands in her lap. But Laura climbed on to Pa's knee and beat him with her fists. 'Where is it? Where is it? Where's my present?' she said, beating him.

Pa laughed his big laugh, like great bells ringing, and he said, 'Why, I do believe there is something in my blouse pocket.'

He took out an oddly shaped package, and very, very slowly he opened it.

'You first, Mary,' he said, 'because you are so patient.' And he gave Mary a comb for her hair. 'And here, flutterbudget! this is for you,' he said to Laura.

The combs were exactly alike. They were made of black rubber and curved to fit over the top of a little girl's head. And over the top of the comb lay a flat piece of black rubber, with curving Slits cut in it, and in the very middle of it a little five-pointed star was cut out. A bright coloured ribbon was drawn underneath, and the colour showed through.

The ribbon in Mary's comb was blue, and the ribbon in Laura's comb was red.

Ma smoothed back their hair and slid the combs into it, and there in the golden hair, exactly over the middle of Mary's forehead, was a little blue star. And in Laura's brown hair, over the middle of her forehead, was a little red star.

Laura looked at Mary's star, and Mary looked at Laura's, and they laughed with joy. They had never had anything so pretty.

Ma said, 'But, Charles, you didn't get yourself a thing!'

'Oh, I got myself a plough,' said Pa. 'Warm weather'll be here soon now, and I'll be ploughing.'

That was the happiest supper they had had for a long time. Pa was safely home again. The fried salt pork was very good, after so many months of eating ducks and geese and turkeys and venison. And nothing had ever tasted so good as those crackers and the little green sour pickles.

Pa told them about all the seeds. He had got seeds of turnips and carrots and onions and cabbage. He had got peas and beans. And corn and wheat and tobacco and the seed potatoes. And water-melon seeds. He said to Ma, 'I tell you, Caroline, when we begin getting crops off this rich land of ours, we'll be living like kings!'

They had almost forgotten the noise from the Indian camp. The window shutters were closed now, and the wind was moaning in the chimney and whining around the house. They were so used to the wind that they did not hear it. But when the wind was silent an instant, Laura heard again that wild, shrill, fast-beating sound from the Indian camps.

Then Pa said something to Ma that made Laura sit very still and listen carefully. He said that folks in Independence said that the government was going to put the white settlers out of the Indian territory. He said the Indians had been complaining and they had got that answer from Washington.

'Oh, Charles, no!' Ma said. 'Not when we have done so much.'

Pa said he didn't believe it. He said, 'They always have let settlers keep the land. They'll make the Indians move on again. Didn't I get word straight from Washington that this country's going to be opened for settlement any time now?'

'I wish they'd settle it and stop talking about it,' Ma said.

After Laura was in bed she lay awake a long time, and so did Mary. Pa and Ma sat in the firelight and candlelight, reading. Pa had brought a newspaper from Kansas, and he read it to Ma. It proved that he was right, the government would not do anything to the white settlers.

Whenever the sound of the wind died away, Laura could faintly hear the noise of that wild jamboree in the Indian camp. Sometimes even above the howling of the wind she thought she still heard those fierce yells of jubilation. Faster, faster, faster they made her heart beat. 'Hi! Hi! Hi-yi! Hah! Hi! Hah!'

22

Prairie Fire

Spring had come. The warm winds smelled exciting, and all outdoors was large and bright and sweet. Big white shining clouds floated high up in clear space. Their shadows floated over the prairie. The shadows were thin and brown, and all the rest of the prairie was the pale, soft colours of dead grasses.

Pa was breaking the prairie sod, with Pet and Patty hitched to the breaking-plough. The sod was a tough, thick mass of grass-roots. Pet and Patty slowly pulled with all their might and the sharp plough slowly turned over a long, unbroken strip of that sod.

The dead grass was so tall and thick that it held up the sod. Where Pa had ploughed, he didn't have a ploughed field. The long strips of grass-roots lay on top of grass, and grass stuck out between them.

But Pa and Pet and Patty kept on working. He said that sod potatoes and sod corn would grow this year, and next year the roots and the dead grasses would be rotted. In two or three years he would have nicely ploughed fields. Pa liked the land because it was so rich, and there wasn't a tree or a stump or a rock in it.

Now a great many Indians came riding along the Indian trail. Indians were everywhere. Their guns echoed in the creek bottoms where they were hunting. No one knew how many Indians were hidden in the prairie which seemed so level but wasn't. Often Laura saw an Indian where no one had been an instant before.

Indians often came to the house. Some were friendly, some were surly and cross. All of them wanted food and tobacco, and Ma gave them what they wanted. She was afraid not to. When an Indian pointed at something and grunted, Ma gave him that thing. But most of the food was kept hidden and locked up.

Jack was cross all the time, even with Laura. He was never let off the chain, and all the time he lay and hated the Indians. Laura and Mary were quite used to seeing them now. Indians didn't surprise them at all. But they always felt safer near Pa or Jack.

One day they were helping Ma get dinner. Baby Carrie was playing on the floor in the sunshine, and suddenly the sunshine was gone.

'I do believe it is going to storm,' Ma said, looking out of the window. Laura looked, too, and great black clouds were billowing up in the south, across the sun.

Pet and Patty were coming running from the field, Pa holding to the heavy plough and bounding in long leaps behind it.

'Prairie fire!' he shouted. 'Get the tub full of water! Put sacks in it! Hurry!'

Ma ran to the well, Laura ran to tug the tub to it. Pa tied Pet to the house. He brought the cow and calf from the picket-line and shut them in the stable. He caught Bunny and tied her fast to the north corner of the house. Ma was pulling up buckets of water as fast as she could. Laura ran to get the sacks that Pa had flung out of the stable.

Pa was ploughing, shouting at Pet and Patty to make them hurry. The sky was black now, the air was as dark as if the sun had set. Pa ploughed a long furrow west of the house and south of the house, and back again east of the house. Rabbits came bounding past him as if he wasn't there.

Pet and Patty came galloping, the plough and Pa bounding behind them. Pa tied them to the other north corner of the house. The tub was full of water. Laura helped Ma push the sacks under the water to soak them.

'I couldn't plough but one furrow; there isn't time,' Pa said. 'Hurry, Caroline. That fire's coming faster than a horse can run.'

A big rabbit bounded right over the tub while Pa and Ma were lifting it. Ma told Laura to stay at the house. Pa and Ma ran staggering to the furrow with the tub.

Laura stayed close to the house. She could see the red fire coming under the billows of smoke. More rabbits went leaping by. They paid no attention to Jack and he didn't think about them; he stared at the red undersides of the rolling smoke and shivered and whined while he crowded close to Laura.

The wind was rising and wildly screaming. Thousands of birds flew before the fire, thousands of rabbits were running.

Pa was going along the furrow, setting fire to the grass on the other side of it. Ma followed with a wet sack, beating at the flames that tried to cross the furrow. The whole prairie was hopping with rabbits. Snakes rippled across the yard. Prairie hens ran silently, their necks outstretched and their wings spread. Birds screamed in the screaming wind.

Pa's little fire was all around the house now, and he helped Ma fight it with the wet sacks. The fire blew wildly, snatching at the dry grass inside the furrow. Pa and Ma thrashed at it with the sacks, when it got across the furrow they stamped it with their feet. They ran back and forth in the smoke, fighting that fire.

The prairie fire was roaring now, roaring louder and louder in the screaming wind. Great flames came roaring, flaring and twisting high. Twists of flame broke loose and came down on the wind to blaze up in the grasses far ahead of the roaring wall of fire. A red light came from the rolling black clouds of smoke overhead.

Mary and Laura stood against the house and held hands and trembled. Baby Carrie was in the house. Laura wanted to do something, but inside her head was a roaring and whirling like the fire. Her middle shook, and tears poured out of her stinging eyes. Her eyes and her nose and her throat stung with smoke.

Jack howled. Bunny and Pet and Patty were jerking at the ropes and squealing horribly. The orange, yellow, terrible flames were coming faster than horses can run, and their quivering light danced over everything.

Pa's little fire had made a burned black strip. The little fire went backing slowly away against the wind, it went slowly crawling to meet the racing furious big fire. And suddenly the big fire swallowed the little one.

The wind rose to a high, crackling, rushing shriek, flames climbed into the crackling air. Fire was all around the house.

Then it was over. The fire went roaring past and away.

Pa and Ma were beating out little fires here and there in the yard. When they were all out, Ma came to the house to wash her hands and face. She was all streaked with smoke and sweat, and she was trembling.

She said there was nothing to worry about. 'The backfire saved us,' she said, 'and all's well that ends well.'

The air smelled scorched. And to the very edge of the sky, the prairie was burned naked and black. Threads of smoke rose from it. Ashes blew on the wind. Everything felt different and miserable. But Pa and Ma were cheerful because the fire was gone and it had not done any harm.

Pa said that the fire had not missed them far, but a miss is as good as a mile. He asked Ma, 'If it had come while I was in Independence, what would you have done?'

'We would have gone to the creek with the birds and the rabbits, of course,' Ma said.

All the wild things on the prairie had known what to do. They ran and flew and hopped and crawled as fast as they could go, to the water that would keep them safe from fire. Only the little soft striped gophers had gone down deep into their holes, and they were the first to come up and look around at the bare, smoking prairie.

Then out of the creek bottoms the birds came flying over it, and a rabbit cautiously hopped and looked. It was a long, long time before the snakes crawled out of the bottoms and the prairie hens came walking.

The fire had gone out among the bluffs. It had never reached the creek bottoms or the Indian camps.

That night Mr Edwards and Mr Scott came to see Pa. They were worried because they thought that perhaps the Indians had started that fire on purpose to burn out the white settlers.

Pa didn't believe it. He said the Indians had always burned the prairie to make green grass grow more quickly, and travelling easier. Their ponies couldn't gallop through the thick, tall, dead grass. Now the ground was clear. And he was glad of it, because ploughing would be easier.

While they were talking, they could hear drums beating in the Indian camps, and shouts. Laura sat still as a mouse on the doorstep and listened to the talk and to the Indians. The stars hung low and large and quivering over the burned prairie, and the wind blew gently in Laura's hair.

Mr Edwards said there were too many Indians in those camps; he didn't like it. Mr Scott said he didn't know why so many of those savages were coming together, if they didn't mean devilment.

'The only good Indian is a dead Indian,' Mr Scott said.

Pa said he didn't know about that. He figured that Indians would be as peaceable as anybody else if they were let alone. On the other hand, they had been moved west so many times that naturally they hated white folks. But an Indian ought to have sense enough to know when he was licked. With soldiers at Fort Gibson and Fort Dodge, Pa didn't believe these Indians would make any trouble.

'As to why they are congregating in these camps, Scott, I can tell you that,' he said. 'They're getting ready for their big spring buffalo hunt.'

He said there were half a dozen tribes down in those camps. Usually the tribes were fighting each other, but every spring they made peace and all came together for the big hunt.

'They're sworn to peace among themselves,' he said, 'and they're thinking about hunting the buffalo. So it's not likely they'll start on the warpath against us. They'll have their talks and their feasts, and then one day they'll all hit the trail after the buffalo herds. The buffalo will be working their way north pretty soon, following the green grass. By George! I'd like to go on a hunt like that myself. It must be a sight to see.'

'Well, maybe you're right about it, Ingalls,' Mr Scott said slowly. 'Anyway, I'll be glad to tell Mrs Scott what you say. She can't get the Minnesota massacres out of her head.'

23

Indian War-Cry

Next morning Pa went whistling to his ploughing. He came in at noon black with soot from the burned prairie, but he was pleased. The tall grass didn't bother him any more.

But there was an uneasiness about the Indians. More and more Indians were in the creek bottoms. Mary and Laura saw the smoke from their fires by day, and at night they heard the savage voices shouting.

Pa came early from the field. He did the chores early, and shut Pet and Patty, Bunny and the cow and calf into the stable. They could not stay out in the yard to graze in the cool moonlight.

When shadows began to gather on the prairie and the wind was quiet, the noises from the Indian camps grew louder and wilder. Pa brought Jack into the house. The door was shut and the latch-string pulled in. No one could go out-doors till morning.

Night crept towards the little house, and the darkness was frightening. It yelped with Indian yells, and one night it began to throb with Indian drums.

In her sleep Laura heard all the time that savage yipping and the wild, throbbing drums. She heard Jack's claws click-ing, and his low growl. Sometimes Pa sat up in bed, listen-ing.

One evening he took his bullet-mould from the box under the bed. He sat for a long time on the hearth, melting lead and making bullets. He did not stop till he had used the last bit of lead.

Laura and Mary lay awake and watched him. He had never made so many bullets at one time before. Mary asked, 'What makes you do that, Pa?'

'Oh, I haven't anything else to do,' Pa said, and he began to whistle cheerfully. But he had been ploughing all day. He was too tired to play the fiddle. He might have gone to bed, instead of sitting up so late, making bullets.

No more Indians came to the house. For days, Mary and Laura had not seen a single Indian. Mary did not like to go out of the house any more. Laura had to play outdoors by herself, and she had a queer feeling about the prairie. It didn't feel safe. It seemed to be hiding something. Sometimes Laura had a feeling that something was watching her, something was creeping up behind her. She turned around quickly, and nothing was there.

Mr Scott and Mr Edwards, with their guns, came and talked to Pa in the field. They talked quite a while, then they went away together. Laura was disappointed because Mr Edwards did not come to the house.

At dinner Pa said to Ma that some of the settlers were talking about a stockade. Laura didn't know what a stockade was. Pa had told Mr Scott and Mr Edwards that it was a foolish notion. He told Ma, 'If we need one, we'd need it before we could get it built. And the last thing we want to do is to act like we're afraid.'

Mary and Laura looked at each other. They knew it was no use to ask questions. They would only be told again that children must not speak at table until they were spoken to. Or that children should be seen and not heard.

That afternoon Laura asked Ma what a stockade was.

Ma said it was something to make little girls ask questions. That meant that grown-ups would not tell you what it was. And Mary looked a look at Laura that said, 'I told you so.'

Laura didn't know why Pa said he must not act as if he were afraid. Pa was never afraid. Laura didn't want to act as if she were afraid, but she was. She was afraid of the Indians.

Jack never laid back his ears and smiled at Laura any more. Even while she petted him, his ears were lifted, his neck bristled, and his lips twitched back from his teeth. His eyes were angry. Every night he growled more fiercely, and every night the Indian drums beat faster, faster, and the wild yipping rose higher and higher, faster, wilder.

In the middle of the night Laura sat straight up and screamed. Some terrible sound had made cold sweat come out all over her.

Ma came to her quickly and said in her gentle way 'Be quiet, Laura. You mustn't frighten Carrie.'

Laura clung to Ma, and Ma was wearing her dress. The fire was covered with ashes and the house was dark, but Ma had not gone to bed. Moonlight came through the window. The shutter was open, and Pa stood in the dark by the window, looking out. He had his gun.

Out in the night the drums were beating and the Indians were wildly yelling.

Then that terrible sound came again. Laura felt as if she were falling; she couldn't hold on to anything; there was nothing solid anywhere. It seemed a long time before she could see or think or speak.

She screamed: 'What is it? What is it? Oh, Pa, what is it?'

She was shaking all over and she felt sick in her middle. She heard the drums pounding and the wild yipping yells and she felt Ma holding her safe. Pa said, 'It's the Indian war-cry, Laura.'

Ma made a soft sound, and he said to her, 'They might as well know, Caroline.'

He explained to Laura that that was the Indian way of talking about war. The Indians were only talking about it, and dancing around their fires. Mary and Laura must not be afraid, because Pa was there, and Jack was there, and soldiers were at Fort Gibson and Fort Dodge.

'So don't be afraid, Mary and Laura,' he said again.

Laura gasped and said, 'No, Pa.' But she was horribly afraid. Mary couldn't say anything; she lay shivering under the covers.

Then Carrie began to cry, so Ma carried her to the rocking-chair and gently rocked her. Laura crept out of bed and huddled against Ma's knee. And Mary, left all alone, crept after her and huddled close, too. Pa stayed by the window, watching.

The drums seemed to beat in Laura's head. They seemed to beat deep inside her. The wild, fast yipping yells were worse than wolves. Something worse was coming, Laura knew it. Then it came—the Indian war-cry.

A nightmare is not so terrible as that night was. A nightmare is only a dream, and when it is worst you wake up. But this was real and Laura could not wake up. She could not get away from it.

When the war-cry was over, Laura knew it had not got her yet. She was still in the dark house and she was pressed close against Ma. Ma was trembling all over. Jack's howling ended in a sobbing growl. Carrie began to scream again, and Pa wiped his forehead and said, 'Whew!'

'I never heard anything like it,' Pa said. He asked, 'How do you suppose they learned to do it?' but nobody answered that.

'They don't need guns. That yell's enough to scare anybody to death,' he said. 'My mouth's so dry I couldn't whistle a tune to save my life. Bring me some water, Laura.'

That made Laura feel better. She carried a dipper full of water to Pa at the window. He took it and smiled at her, and that made her feel very much better. He drank a little and smiled again and said, 'There! now I can whistle!'

He whistled a few notes to show her that he could.

Then he listened. And Laura, too, heard far away the soft pitter-pat, pat-pat, pitter-pat pat, of a pony's galloping. It came nearer.

From one side of the house came the drum-throbbing and the fast, shrill, yapping yells, and from the other side came the lonely sound of the rider's galloping.

Nearer and nearer it came. Now the hoofs clattered loudly and suddenly they were going by. The galloping went by and grew fainter, down the creek road.

In the moonlight Laura saw the behind of a little black Indian pony, and an Indian on its back. She saw a huddle of blanket and a naked head and a flutter of feathers above it, and moonlight on a gun barrel and then it was all gone. Nothing was there but empty prairie.

Pa said he was durned if he knew what to make of it. He said that was the Osage who had tried to talk French to him.

He asked, 'What's he doing, out at this hour, riding hell bent for leather?'

Nobody answered because nobody knew.

The drums throbbed and the Indians went on yelling. The terrible war-cry came again and again.

Little by little, after a long time, the yells grew fainter and fewer. At last Carrie cried herself to sleep. Ma sent Mary and Laura back to bed.

Next day they could not go out of the house. Pa stayed close by. There was not one sound from the Indian camps. The whole vast prairie was still. Only the wind blew over the blackened earth where there was no grass to rustle. The wind blew past the house with a rushing sound like running water.

That night the noise in the Indian camps was worse than the night before. Again the war-cries were more terrible than the most dreadful nightmare. Laura and Mary huddled close against Ma, poor little Baby Carrie cried, Pa watched at the window with his gun. And all night long Jack paced and growled, and screamed when the war-cries came.

The next night, and the next night, and the next night, were worse and worse. Mary and Laura were so tired that they fell asleep while the drums pounded and the Indians yelled. But a war-cry always jerked them wide awake in terror.

And the silent days were even worse than the nights. Pa watched and listened all the time. The plough was in the field where he had left it; Pet and Patty and the colt and the cow and calf stayed in the barn. Mary and Laura could not go out of the house. And Pa never stopped looking at the prairie all around, and turning his head quickly towards the smallest noise. He ate hardly any dinner; he kept getting up and going outdoors to look all around at the prairie.

One day his head nodded down to the table and he slept there. Ma and Mary and Laura were still to let him sleep. He was so tired. But in a minute he woke up with a jump and said, sharply, to Ma, 'Don't let me do that again!'

'Jack was on guard,' Ma said gently.

That night was worst of all. The drums were faster and the yells were louder and fiercer. All up and down the creek war-cries answered war-cries and the bluffs echoed. There was no rest. Laura ached all over and there was a terrible ache in her very middle.

At the window Pa said, 'Caroline, they are quarrelling among themselves. Maybe they will fight each other.'

'Oh, Charles, if they only will!' Ma said.

All night there was not a minute's rest. Just before dawn a last war-cry ended and Laura slept against Ma's knee.

She woke up in bed. Mary was sleeping beside her. The door was open, and by the sunshine on the floor Laura knew it was almost noon. Ma was cooking dinner. Pa sat on the doorstep.

He said to Ma, 'There's another big party, going off to the south.'

Laura went to the door in her nightgown, and she saw a long line of Indians far away. The line came up out of the black prairie and it went farther away southward. The Indians on their ponies were so small in the distance that they looked not much bigger than ants.

Pa said that two big parties of Indians had gone west that morning. Now this one was going south. It meant that the Indians had quarrelled among themselves. They were going away from their camps in the creek bottoms. They would not go all together to their big buffalo-hunt.

That night the darkness came quietly. There was no sound except the rushing of the wind.

'Tonight we'll sleep!' Pa said, and they did. All night long they did not even dream. And in the morning Jack was still sleeping limp and flat on the same spot where he had been sleeping when Laura went to bed.

The next night was still, too, and again they all slept soundly. That morning Pa said he felt as fresh as a daisy, and he was going to do a little scouting along the creek.

He chained Jack to the ring in the house wall, and he took his gun and went out of sight down the creek road.

Laura and Mary and Ma could not do anything but wait until he came back. They stayed in the house and wished he would come. The sunshine had never moved so slowly on the floor as it did that day.

But he did come back. Late in the afternoon he came. And everything was all right. He had gone far up and down the creek and had seen many deserted Indian camps. All the Indians had gone away, except a tribe called the Osages.

In the woods Pa had met an Osage who could talk to him. This Indian told him that all the tribes except the Osages had made up their minds to kill the white people who had come into the Indian country. And they were getting ready to do it when the lone Indian came riding into their big pow-wow.

That Indian had come riding so far and fast because he did not want them to kill the white people. He was an Osage, and they called him a name that meant he was a great soldier.

'Soldat du Chêne', Pa said his name was.

'He kept arguing with them day and night,' Pa said, 'till all the other Osages agreed with him. Then he stood up and told the other tribes that if they started to massacre us, the Osages would fight them.'

That was what had made so much noise, that last terrible night. The other tribes were howling at the Osages, and the Osages were howling back at them. The other tribes did not dare fight Soldat du Chêne and all his Osages, so next day they went away.

'That's one good Indian!' Pa said. No matter what Mr Scott said, Pa did not believe that the only good Indian was a dead Indian.

24

Indians Ride Away

There was another long night of sleep. It was so good to lie down and sleep soundly. Everything was safe and quiet. Only the owls called 'Who-oo? Who-oo?' in the woods along the creek, while the great moon sailed slowly over the curve of the sky above the endless prairie.

In the morning the sun shone warmly. Down by the creek the frogs were croaking. 'Garrump! Garrump!' they cried by the edge of the pools. 'Knee deep! Knee deep! Better go 'round.'

Ever since Ma had told them what the frogs were saying, Mary and Laura could hear the words plainly.

The door was open to let in the warm spring air. After breakfast Pa went out, whistling merrily. He was going to hitch Pet and Patty to the plough again. But his whistling suddenly stopped. He stood on the doorstep, looking towards the east, and he said, 'Come here, Caroline. And you, Mary and Laura.'

Laura ran out first, and she was surprised. The Indians were coming.

They did not come on the creek road. They came riding up out of the creek bottoms far to the east.

First came the tall Indian who had gone riding by the house in the moonlight. Jack was growling and Laura's heart beat fast. She was glad to be close to Pa. But she knew this was the good Indian, the Osage chief who had stopped the terrible war-cries.

His black pony came trotting willingly, sniffing the wind that blew its mane and tail like fluttering banners. The pony's nose and head were free; it wore no bridle. Not even one strap was on it anywhere. There was nothing to make it do anything it didn't want to do. Willingly it came trotting along the old Indian trail as if it liked to carry the Indian on its back.

Jack growled savagely, trying to get loose from his chain. He remembered this Indian who had pointed a gun at him. Pa said, 'Be still, Jack.' Jack growled again, and for the first time in their lives Pa struck him. 'Lie down! Be still!' Pa said. Jack cowered down and was still.

The pony was very near now, and Laura's heart beat faster and faster. She looked at the Indian's beaded moccasin, she looked up along the fringed legging that clung to the pony's bare side. A bright-coloured blanket was wrapped around the Indian. One bare brown-red arm carried a rifle lightly across the pony's naked shoulders. Then Laura looked up at the Indian's fierce, still, brown face.

It was a proud, still face. No matter what happened, it would always be like that. Nothing would change it. Only the eyes were alive in that face, and they gazed steadily far away to the west. They did not move. Nothing moved or changed, except the eagle feathers standing straight up from the scalplock on the shaved head. The long feathers swayed and dipped, waving and spinning in the wind as the tall Indian on the black pony passed on into the distance.

'Du Chêne himself,' Pa said, under his breath, and he lifted his hand in salute.

But the happy pony and the motionless Indian went by. They went by as if the house and stable and Pa and Ma and Mary and Laura were not there at all.

Pa and Ma and Mary and Laura slowly turned and looked at that Indian's proud straight back. Then other ponies and other blankets and shaved heads and eagle feathers came between. One by one on the path, more and more savage warriors were riding behind Du Chêne. Brown face after brown face went by. Ponies' manes and tails blew in the wind, beads glittered, fringe flapped, eagle feathers were waving on all the naked heads. Rifles lying on the ponies' shoulders bristled all along the line.

Laura was excited about the ponies. There were black ponies, bay ponies, grey and brown and spotted ponies. Their little feet went trippety-trip-trip, trippety-trip, pat-patter, pat-patter, trippety pat-patter, all along the Indian trail. Their nostrils widened at Jack and their bodies shied away from him, but they came on bravely, looking with their bright eyes at Laura.

'Oh, the pretty ponies! See the pretty ponies!' she cried, clapping her hands. 'Look at the spotted one.'

She thought she would never be tired of watching those ponies coming by, but after a while she began to look at the women and children on their backs. The women and children came riding behind the Indian men. Little naked brown Indians, no bigger than Mary and Laura, were riding the pretty ponies. The ponies did not have to wear bridles or saddles, and the little Indians did not have to wear clothes. All their skin was out in the fresh air and the sunshine. Their straight black hair blew in the wind and their black eyes sparkled with joy. They sat on their ponies stiff and still like grown-up Indians.

Laura looked and looked at the Indian children, and they looked at her. She had a naughty wish to be a little Indian girl. Of course she did not really mean it. She only wanted to be bare naked in the wind and the sunshine, and riding one of those gay little ponies.

The Indian children's mothers were riding ponies, too.

Leather fringe dangled about their legs and blankets were wrapped around their bodies, but the only thing on their heads was their black, smooth hair. Their faces were brown and placid. Some had narrow bundles tied on their backs, and tiny babies' heads stuck out of the top of the bundles. And some babies and some small children rode in baskets hanging at the ponies' sides, beside their mothers.

More and more and more ponies passed, and more children, and more babies on their mothers' backs, and more babies in baskets on the ponies' sides. Then came a mother riding, with a baby in a basket on each side of her pony.

Laura looked straight into the bright eyes of the little baby nearer her. Only its small head showed above the basket's rim. Its hair was as black as a crow and its eyes were black as a night when no stars shine.

Those black eyes looked deep into Laura's eyes and she looked deep down into the blackness of that little baby's eyes, and she wanted that one little baby.

'Pa,' she said, 'get me that little Indian baby!'

'Hush, Laura!' Pa told her sternly.

The little baby was going by. Its head turned and its eyes kept looking into Laura's eyes.

'Oh, I want it! I want it!' Laura begged. The baby was going farther and farther away, but it did not stop looking back at Laura. 'It wants to stay with me,' Laura begged. 'Please, Pa, please!'

'Hush, Laura,' Pa said. 'The Indian woman wants to keep her baby.'

'Oh, Pa!' Laura pleaded, and then she began to cry. It was shameful to cry, but she couldn't help it. The little Indian baby was gone. She knew she would never see it any more.

Ma said she had never heard of such a thing. 'For shame, Laura,' she said, but Laura could not stop crying. 'Why on earth do you want an Indian baby, of all things?' Ma asked her.

'Its eyes are so black,' Laura sobbed. She could not say what she meant.

'Why, Laura,' Ma said, 'you don't want another baby. We have a baby, our own baby.'

'I want the other one, too!' Laura sobbed, loudly.

'Well, I declare!' Ma exclaimed.

'Look at the Indians, Laura,' said Pa. 'Look west, and then look east, and see what you see.'

Laura could hardly see at first. Her eyes were full of tears and sobs kept jerking out of her throat. But she obeyed Pa as best she could, and in a moment she was still. As far as she could see to the west and as far as she could see to the east there were Indians. There was no end to that long, long line.

'That's an awful lot of Indians,' Pa said.

More and more and more Indians came riding by. Baby Carrie grew tired of looking at Indians and played by herself on the floor. But Laura sat on the doorstep, Pa stood close beside her, and Ma and Mary stood in the doorway. They looked and looked and looked at Indians riding by.

It was dinner-time, and no one thought of dinner. Indian ponies were still going by, carrying bundles of skins and tent-poles and dangling baskets and cooking pots. There were a few more women and a few more naked Indian children. Then the very last pony went by. But Pa and Ma and Laura and Mary still stayed in the doorway, looking, till that long line of Indians slowly pulled itself over the western edge of the world. And nothing was left but silence and emptiness. All the world seemed very quiet and lonely.

Ma said she didn't feel like doing anything, she was so let down. Pa told her not to do anything but rest.

'You must eat something, Charles,' Ma said.

'No,' said Pa. 'I don't feel hungry.' He went soberly to

hitch up Pet and Patty, and he began again to break the tough sod with the plough.

Laura could not eat anything, either. She sat a long time on the doorstep, looking into the empty west where the Indians had gone. She seemed still to see waving feathers and black eyes and to hear the sound of ponies' feet.

25

Soldiers

After the indians had gone, a great peace settled on the prairie. And one morning the whole land was green.

'When did that grass grow?' Ma asked, in amazement. 'I thought the whole country was black, and now there's nothing but green grass as far as the eye can see.'

The whole sky was filled with lines of wild ducks and wild geese flying north. Crows cawed above the trees along the creek. The winds whispered in the new grass, bringing scents of earth and of growing things.

In the mornings the meadow larks rose singing into the sky. All day the curlews and killdeers and sandpipers chirped and sang in the creek bottoms. Often in the early evening the mocking-birds were singing.

One night Pa and Mary and Laura sat still on the doorstep, watching little rabbits playing in the grass in the starlight. Three rabbit mothers hopped about with lopping ears and watched their little rabbits playing, too.

In the daytime everyone was busy. Pa hurried with his ploughing, and Mary and Laura helped Ma plant the early garden seeds. With the hoe Ma dug small holes in the matted grass roots that the plough had turned up, and Laura and Mary carefully dropped the seeds. Then Ma covered them snugly with earth. They planted onions and carrots and peas and beans and turnips. And they were all so happy because spring had come, and pretty soon they would have vegetables to eat. They were growing very tired of just bread and meat.

One evening Pa came from the field before sunset and he helped Ma set out the cabbage plants and the sweet potato plants. Ma had sowed the cabbage seed in a flat box and kept it in the house. She watered it carefully, and carried it every day from the morning sunshine to the afternoon sunshine that came through the windows. And she had saved one of the Christmas sweet potatoes, and planted it in another box. The cabbage seeds were now little grey-green plants, and the sweet potato had sent up a stem and green leaves from every one of its eyes.

Pa and Ma took each tiny plant very carefully and settled its roots comfortably in holes made for them. They watered the roots and pressed earth upon them firmly. It was dark before the last plant was in its place, and Pa and Ma were tired. But they were glad, too, because this year they'd have cabbages and sweet potatoes.

Every day they all looked at that garden. It was rough and grassy because it was made in the prairie sod, but all the tiny plants were growing. Little crumpled leaves of peas came up, and tiny spears of onions. The beans themselves popped out of the ground. But it was a little yellow bean-stem, coiled like a spring, that pushed them up. Then the bean was cracked open and dropped by two baby bean-leaves, and the leaves unfolded flat to the sunshine.

Pretty soon they would all begin to live like kings.

Every morning Pa went cheerfully whistling to the field. He had planted some early sod potatoes, and some potatoes were saved to plant later. Now he carried a sack of corn fastened to his belt, and as he ploughed he threw grains of corn into the furrow beside the plough's point. The plough turned over a strip of sod on top of the seed corn. But the corn would fight its way up through the matted roots, and there would be a cornfield.

There would be green corn for dinner some day. And next winter there would be ripe corn for Pet and Patty to eat.

One morning Mary and Laura were washing the dishes and Ma was making the beds. She was humming softly to herself and Laura and Mary were talking about the garden. Laura liked peas best, and Mary liked beans. Suddenly they heard Pa's voice, loud and angry.

Ma went quickly to the door, and Laura and Mary peeped out on either side of her.

Pa was driving Pet and Patty from the field, dragging the plough behind them. Mr Scott and Mr Edwards were with Pa, and Mr Scott was talking earnestly.

'No, Scott!' Pa answered him. 'I'll not stay here to be taken away by the soldiers like an outlaw! If some blasted politicians in Washington hadn't sent out word it would be all right to settle here, I'd never have been three miles over the line into Indian Territory. But I'll not wait for the soldiers to take us out. We're going now!'

'What is the matter, Charles? Where are we going?' Ma asked.

'Durned if I know! But we're going. We're leaving here!' Pa said. 'Scott and Edwards say the government is sending soldiers to take all us settlers out of Indian Territory.'

His face was very red and his eyes were like blue fire. Laura was frightened; she had never seen Pa look like that. She pressed close against Ma and was still, looking at Pa.

Mr Scott started to speak, but Pa stopped him. 'Save your breath, Scott. It's no use to say another word. You can stay till the soldiers come if you want to. I'm going out now.'

Mr Edwards said he was going, too. He would not stay to be driven across the line like an ornery yellow hound.

'Ride out to Independence with us, Edwards,' Pa said. But Mr Edwards answered that he didn't care to go north.

He would make a boat and go on down the river to some settlement farther south.

'Better come out with us,' Pa urged him, 'and go down on foot through Missouri. It's a risky trip, one man alone in a boat, going down the Verdigris among the wild Indian tribes.'

But Mr Edwards said he had already seen Missouri and he had plenty of powder and lead.

Then Pa told Mr Scott to take the cow and calf. 'We can't take them with us,' Pa said. 'You've been a good neighbour, Scott, and I'm sorry to leave you. But we're going out in the morning.'

Laura heard all this, but she had not believed it until she saw Mr Scott leading away the cow. The gentle cow went meekly away with the rope around her long horns, and the calf frisked and jumped behind. There went all the milk and butter.

Mr Edwards said he would be too busy to see them again. He shook hands with Pa, saying, 'Good-bye, Ingalls, and good luck.' He shook hands with Ma and said, 'Good-bye, ma'am. I won't be seeing you all again, but I sure will never forget your kindness.'

Then he turned to Mary and Laura, and he shook their hands as if they were grown up. 'Good-bye,' he said.

Mary said, politely, 'Good-bye, Mr Edwards.' But Laura forgot to be polite. She said: 'Oh, Mr Edwards, I wish you wouldn't go away! Oh, Mr Edwards, thank you, thank you for going all the way to Independence to find Santa Claus for us.'

Mr Edwards' eyes shone very bright, and he went away without saying another word.

Pa began to unhitch Pet and Patty in the middle of the morning, and Laura and Mary knew it was really true; they really were going away from there. Ma didn't say anything. She went into the house and looked around, at the dishes not washed and the bed only partly made, and she lifted up both hands and sat down.

Mary and Laura went on doing the dishes. They were careful not to let them make a sound. They turned around quickly when Pa came in.

He looked like himself again, and he was carrying the potato-sack.

'Here you are, Caroline!' he said, and his voice sounded natural. 'Cook a plenty for dinner! We've been going without potatoes, saving them for seed. Now we'll eat 'em up!'

So that day for dinner they ate the seed potatoes. They were very good, and Laura knew that Pa was right when he said, 'There's no great loss without some small gain.'

After dinner he took the wagon bows from their pegs in the barn. He put them on the wagon, one end of each bow in its iron strap on one side of the wagon box, and the other end in its iron strap on the other side. When all the bows were standing up in their places, Pa and Ma spread the wagon cover over them and tied it down tightly. Then Pa pulled the rope in the end of the wagon cover till it puckered together and left only a tiny round hole in the middle of the back.

There stood the covered wagon, all ready to load in the morning.

Everyone was quiet that night. Even Jack felt that something was wrong, and he lay down close to Laura when she went to bed.

It was now too warm for a fire, but Pa and Ma sat looking at the ashes in the fireplace.

Ma sighed gently and said, 'A whole year gone, Charles.' But Pa answered cheerfully: 'What's a year amount to? We have all the time there is.'

26

Going Out

After breakfast next morning, Pa and Ma packed the wagon. First of all the bedding was made into two beds, laid on top of each other across the back of the wagon, and carefully covered with a pretty plaid blanket. Mary and Laura and Baby Carrie would ride there in the daytime. At night the top bed would be put in the front of the wagon, for Pa and Ma to sleep in. And Mary and Laura would sleep in the bottom bed, where it was.

Next Pa took the small cupboard from the wall, and in it Ma packed the food and the dishes. Pa put the cupboard under the wagon-seat, and in front of it he laid a sack of corn for the horses.

'It will make a good rest for our feet, Caroline,' he said to Ma.

Ma packed all the clothing in two carpet-bags, and Pa hung them to the wagon bows inside the wagon. Opposite them he hung his rifle in its straps, and his bullet-pouch and powder-horn hung beneath it. His fiddle in its box he laid on one end of the bed, where it would ride softly.

Ma wrapped the black iron spider, the bake-ven, and the coffee-pot in sacks, and put them in the wagon, while Pa tied the rocking-hair and the tub outside, and hung the water-bucket and the horse-bucket underneath. And he put the tin lantern carefully in the front corner of the wagon-box, where the sack of corn held it still.

Now the wagon was loaded. The only thing they could not take was the plough. Well, that could not be helped. There was no room for it. When they came to wherever they were going, Pa could get more furs to trade for another plough.

Laura and Mary climbed into the wagon and sat on the bed in the back. Ma put Baby Carrie between them. They were all freshly washed and combed. Pa said they were clean as a hound's tooth, and Ma told them they were bright as new pins.

Then Pa hitched Pet and Patty to the wagon. Ma climbed to her place on the seat and held the lines. And suddenly Laura wanted to see the house again. She asked Pa please to let her look out. So he loosened the rope in the back of the wagon-cover, and that made a large round hole. Laura and Mary could look out of it, but still the rope held up enough canvas to keep Carrie from tumbling into the feed-box.

The snug log house looked just as it always had. It did not seem to know they were going away. Pa stood a moment in the doorway and looked all around inside; he looked at the bedstead and the fireplace and the glass windows. Then he closed the door carefully, leaving the latch-string out.

'Someone might need shelter,' he said.

He climbed to his place beside Ma, gathered the reins into his own hands, and chirruped to Pet and Patty.

Jack went under the wagon. Pet whinnied to Bunny, who came to walk beside her. And they were off.

Just before the creek road went down into the bottoms, Pa stopped the mustangs, and they all looked back.

As far as they could see, to the east and to the south and to the west, nothing was moving on all the vastness of the High Prairie. Only the green grass was rippling in the wind, and white clouds drifted in the high, clear sky.

'It's a great country, Caroline,' Pa said. 'But there will be wild Indians and wolves here for many a long day.'

The little log house and the little stable sat lonely in the stillness.

Then Pet and Patty briskly started onward. The wagon went down from the bluffs into the wooded creek bottoms, and high in a tree-top a mocking-bird began to sing.

'I never heard a mocking-bird sing so early,' said Ma, and Pa answered softly, 'He is telling us good-bye.'

They rode down through the low hills to the creek. The ford was low, an easy crossing. On they went, across the bottoms where antlered deer stood up to watch them passing, and mother deer with their fawns bounded into the shadows of the woods. And up between the steep redearth cliffs the wagon climbed to prairie again.

Pet and Patty were eager to go. Their hoofs had made a muffled sound in the bottoms, but now they rang on the hard prairie. And the wind sang shrill against the foremost wagon bows.

Pa and Ma were still and silent on the wagon-seat, and Mary and Laura were quiet, too. But Laura felt all excited inside. You never know what will happen next, nor where you'll be tomorrow, when you are travelling in a covered wagon.

At noon Pa stopped beside a little spring to let the mustangs eat and drink and rest. The spring would soon be dry in the summer's heat, but there was plenty of water now.

Ma took cold cornbread and meat from the food-box, and they all ate, sitting on the clean grass in the shade of the wagon. They drank from the spring, and Laura and Mary ran around in the grass, picking wild flowers, while Ma tidied the food-box and Pa hitched up Pet and Patty again.

Then for a long time they went on, across the prairie. There was nothing to be seen but the blowing grass, the sky, and the endless wagon track. Now and then a rabbit bounded away. Sometimes a prairie hen with her brood of prairie chicks scuttled out of sight in the grass. Baby Carrie slept, and Mary and

Laura were almost asleep when they heard Pa say, 'Something's wrong there.'

Laura jumped up, and far ahead on the prairie she saw a small, light-coloured bump. She couldn't see anything else unusual.

'Where?' she asked Pa.

'There,' Pa said, nodding towards that bump. 'It isn't moving.'

Laura didn't say any more. She kept on looking, and she saw that that bump was a covered wagon. Slowly it grew bigger. She saw that no horses were hitched to it. Nothing moved, anywhere around it. Then she saw something dark in front of it.

The dark thing was two people sitting on the wagon tongue. They were a man and a woman. They sat looking down at their feet, and they moved only their heads to look up when Pet and Patty stopped in front of them.

'What's wrong? Where are your horses?' Pa asked.

'I don't know,' the man said. 'I tied them to the wagon last night, and this morning they were gone. Somebody cut the ropes and took them away in the night.'

'What about your dog?' said Pa.

'Haven't got a dog,' the man said.

Jack stayed under the wagon. He didn't growl, but he didn't come out. He was a sensible dog, and knew what to do when he met strangers.

'Well, your horses are gone,' Pa told the man. 'You'll never see them again. Hanging's too good for horsethieves.'

'Yes,' the man said.

Pa looked at Ma, and Ma barely nodded. Then Pa said, 'Come ride with us to Independence.'

'No,' said the man. 'All we've got is in this wagon. We won't leave it.'

'Why, man! What will you do?' Pa exclaimed. 'There may be nobody along here for days, weeks. You can't stay here.'

'I don't know,' the man said.

'We'll stay with our wagon,' the woman said. She was looking down at her hands clasped in her lap, and Laura couldn't see her face; she could see only the side of the sun-bonnet.

'Better come,' Pa told them. 'You can come back for your wagon.'

'No,' the woman said.

They wouldn't leave the wagon; everything they owned in the world was in it. So at last Pa drove on, leaving them sitting on the wagon tongue; all alone on the prairie.

Pa muttered to himself: 'Tenderfeet! Everything they own, and no dog to watch it. Didn't keep watch himself. And tied his horses with ropes!' Pa snorted. 'Tenderfeet!' he said again. 'Shouldn't be allowed loose west of the Mississippi!'

'But, Charles! Whatever will become of them?' Ma asked him.

'There are soldiers at Independence,' said Pa. 'I'll tell the captain, and he'll send out men to bring them in. They can hold out that long. But it's durned lucky for them that we came by. If we hadn't, there's no telling when they would have been found.'

Laura watched that lonely wagon until it was only a small lump on the prairie. Then it was a speck. Then it was gone.

All the rest of that day Pa drove on and on. They didn't see anybody else.

When the sun was setting, Pa stopped by a well. A house had once been there, but it was burned. The well held plenty of good water, and Laura and Mary gathered bits of half-burned wood to make the fire, while Pa unhitched and watered the horses and put them on picketlines. Then Pa took the seat down from the wagon and lifted out the food-box. The fire burned beautifully, and Ma quickly got supper.

Everything was just as it used to be before they built the house. Pa and Ma and Carrie were on the wagon-seat, Laura and Mary sat on the wagon tongue. They ate the good supper, hot from the camp fire. Pet and Patty and Bunny munched the good grass, and Laura saved bits for Jack, who mustn't beg but could eat his fill as soon as supper was over.

Then the sun went down, far away in the west, and it was time to make the camp ready for night.

Pa chained Pet and Patty to the feed-box at the end of the wagon. He chained Bunny to the side. And he fed them all their supper of corn. Then he sat by the fire and smoked his pipe, while Ma tucked Mary and Laura into bed and laid Baby Carrie beside them.

She sat down beside Pa at the fire, and Pa took his fiddle out of its box and began to play.

'Oh, Susanna, don't you cry for me,' the fiddle wailed, and Pa began to sing.

> 'I went to California
>   With my wash-pan on my knee,
> And every time I thought of home,
>   I wished it wasn't me.'

'Do you know, Caroline,' Pa stopped singing to say, 'I've been thinking what fun the rabbits will have, eating that garden we planted.'

'Don't, Charles,' Ma said.

'Never mind, Caroline!' Pa told her. 'We'll make a better garden. Anyway, we're taking more out of Indian Territory than we took in.'

'I don't know what,' Ma said, and Pa answered, 'Why, there's the mule!' Then Ma laughed, and Pa and the fiddle sang again.

> 'In Dixie land I'll take my stand,
> And live and die in Dixie!
> Away, away, away, away,
> Away down south in Dixie!'

They sang with a lilt and a swing that almost lifted Laura right out of bed. She must lie still and not wake Carrie. Mary was sleeping, too, but Laura had never been wider awake.

She heard Jack making his bed under the wagon. He was turning round and round, trampling down the grass. Then he curled into that round nest with a flop and a sigh of satisfaction.

Pet and Patty were munching the last of their corn, and their chains rattled. Bunny lay down beside the wagon.

They were all there together, safe and comfortable for the night, under the wide, starlit sky. Once more the covered wagon was home.

The fiddle began to play a marching tune, and Pa's clear voice was singing like a deep-toned bell.

> 'And we'll rally round the flag, boys,
> We'll rally once again,
> Shouting the battle-cry of Freedom!'

Laura felt that she must shout, too. But softly Ma looked in through the round hole in the wagon-cover.

'Charles,' Ma said, 'Laura is wide awake. She can't go to sleep on such music as that.'

Pa didn't answer, but the voice of the fiddle changed. Softly and slurringly it began a long, swinging rhythm that seemed to rock Laura gently.

She felt her eyelids closing. She began to drift over endless waves of prairie grasses, and Pa's voice went with her, singing.

> 'Row away, row o'er the waters so blue,
> Like a feather we sail in our gum-tree canoe.
> Row the boat lightly, love, over the sea;
> Daily and nightly I'll wander with thee.'

Contents